CAROLYN BALDUCCI

Is there a life after graduation, Henry Birnbaum?

Houghton Mifflin Company Boston 1971

We are grateful to *Ingenue* magazine
for permission to include Part I, Chapter 1 of
this book which they originally published as
a short story under the title HENRY BIRNBAUM,
IS THERE A LIFE AFTER GRADUATION?

LIBRARY OF CONGRESS CATALOG CARD NUMBER 78–163168
ISBN 0–395–12749–1
PRINTED IN THE UNITED STATES OF AMERICA
FIRST PRINTING C

MAY 1 '72

To: Gioacchino and Sirad

Part I

1

Henry Birnbaum is my best friend. But not my only friend. We both do have other friends — mine from the team, his on the school paper. We go to the same school in Queens, New York. It looks like most schools: gray stone façade, tiled halls, johns that are labeled GENTLEMEN and LADIES — the only concession the school makes to what the guidance counselors call our "growing maturity." Anyway, Henry and I are mostly weekend friends — Saturday-afternoon movies in the winter, the long trek by subway to the Cloisters in the spring, Coney Island in the fall. We usually spend Sundays (after family obligations are dispensed with) listening to music together at my house.

Before I go on, I'd better describe Henry. Physically, he's very unusual, probably because he's so smart. He's a Merit Scholar, tops in his class since kindergarten, it seems, and — not to put down that general type of guy — Henry is *intelligent* on top of all that (if you know what I mean). When you look at him from a distance, Henry is mostly head. He has lots of hair on top, and has let his sideburns grow thick, right down to his chin. His body is always hiding under a rumpled outfit purchased at an Army surplus store, and it kind of hangs downward (his body, that is) when he walks, as though he were a sack of potatoes swinging under a pumpkin-sized head. Which is to say that Henry is not so great-looking. (Although my cousin Ida once told me that she thinks he's very "cuddly," wrinkling up her nose when she said it. And I suppose coming from a girl, that was a compliment.) Henry also has some weird idiosyncrasies. For one thing, his hands are never still. In fact, they seem to be the only things with which Henry does not tire of playing. He makes me nervous in stores and museums. A psychologist might say that he has an arrested oral fixation, since he has been seen patiently chewing on his ties, books, chairbacks, and records — mostly records, and usually mine.

As I said, he comes over to my house after Sunday dinner to listen to music and to talk. So today he comes over, and we go to my room where my brother (who is away at Yale) and I have built a fantastic stereo-tape sound system out of kits (it took us four years to get all the components together). Practically everything that makes or made sound is on tapes or records in that room: Churchill, Glenn Miller, Enrico Caruso, The Goon Shows, Elvis, classics, some vintage rock, and, of course, all the current stuff. The Rolling Stones turn Henry on; my tastes, I admit, are less earthy, which is where it's at when I have to deal with Henry. Anyway, Henry drifts into my room; I close the door.

My parents are pretty cool, but they are caught up in their ambivalence over whether the door should be left closed or ajar. On the one hand, they respect my privacy — not to mention their intolerance of rock at the upper decibels. On the other hand, they do read the papers and they do know that there's a lot of grass floating around in Queens. So they compromise by letting us keep the door shut, and then finding excuses for coming in every fifteen or twenty minutes. They're very uptight about this, but they're doing what they're supposed to do, and Henry defends them and all their hang-ups on these grounds. When my father comes in to visit us, he asks all sorts of rhetorical questions ("What do you think violence has ever accomplished?" "Don't you think the poor are partly responsible for their own lives?" "Can't you see that Mark Rudd is just another punk kid?"). But it is my mother whom Henry is in love with. Not because she is so great-looking, but because when she comes in to "visit" us, she brings in apple cider and brownies. I'm not one to look a gift horse in the mouth, but I think that Henry's enthusiasm is probably due to the satisfaction of his sublimated oral desires and the intensification of his inchoate masculine ego. You see, if my father baked brownies and brought them in every twenty minutes Henry might resent the intrusion. But my mother — Jane Fonda, she's not — is still a symbol of a whole new world: women.

So anyway, I'm closing the door. Henry goes straight to the tape deck. He fiddles with it for a minute, turns up the volume, and suddenly Mick Jagger's voice fills the room. "Haannannkee tonk wim-in, gimmee, gimmee, gimmee the honky tonk bluuues . . ." Henry has become transfixed. The sound is penetrating his inner dimensions. I sit down on the floor. For two long minutes Henry doesn't move — not even his fingers. The song flows into its final coda, and the three staccato drumbeats end the trance. I rise to turn down the volume. Even the soundproofing and special flooring don't block the pulsation of beats through our super-uptight neighbors' walls. (They claim their dog gets sick all over their fourteen-dollar-a-square-yard wall-to-wall carpeting. Good Grief!) I turn to Henry after this adjustment, and notice that for the first time in a long while he seems together. He is smiling a crazy smile.

"David," he begins.

"Yes, Henry?"

"Guess what happened yesterday." He is still smiling.

"I have no idea." He smiles some more, which makes me nervous. So I say the least likely thing that comes to my mind, "You met a chick."

His smile evaporates. He blinks. His fingers come

to life. "How did you know?" Then he snaps back into his smile. "But that's not all!"

I am astonished. Henry meeting a chick and being able to smile about it the next day is something new.

"She's a groovy chick — small, long blond hair, pink cheeks, no make-up. I met her at the library." Henry, evidently weakening in the knees, lies down on the other bed. "I told you I was going to the public library."

"Right, to beat your head against the college catalogs."

"Yeah."

"So you met her over C for Cornell or D for Duke?"

"No, I met her outside, at Fifth Avenue and Forty-second Street. She wanted to know which bus to take to get to Washington Square." He positively chuckles. "She's from Ohio!"

"So you showed her St. Mark's Place, took her to the Bleecker Street Cinema, gently helped her step over the bums outside the Village Gate . . ."

"No, man. It was too nice a day. Besides, that scene is beginning to bore me. We went up to Central Park and walked and walked for hours. And we talked. First time I really came out of myself with a girl. She's such a beautiful person. Yes, that's it. She's pretty, but inside she's prettier."

"Sounds nice. You have something going?" I ask with a sharp twinge of what could be jealousy.

"Maybe. We'll see. She has to leave New York this week. Her father is here to attend some conference. But, more important than, you know, 'Will

7

she go steady' and all that rot, she really straightened me out." I shoot him a look from beneath my elbow. "You know how insane this nonsense about college is getting, and how you keep telling me to relax?"

"Yeah."

"And you know how complicated this applying to schools has become for me because I know that no matter where I apply I'll be accepted with a scholarship. Not that that matters. High College Board scores, great potential, newspaper editor, class treasurer. But still, the guidance counselor has to throw me out of his office every Thursday so he can deal with all the dodoes who can't get into any school. David, if you didn't have such a strong preference for science and psychology, you'd be in the same boat. I guess what's really bugging me — I mean, I know you can change your major when you're in school — is that so much is expected of me. Suppose I go to school and grad school and post-grad school and come out a disaster because I choose the wrong college now. My obsession is not my future, actually, but mediocrity. Selecting a college seemed so impossible because I was seeing it as the first decision, the first place to go wrong."

"But you're going to apply to three schools, aren't you?"

"No, man. They'll all accept me. I'll be just as nowhere."

"Henry, you're not making as much sense as you think. You get to go to these places and see them!"

"Suppose one is in California, and one's in England, and one's in Texas?" He sits up on the edge of the bed and starts biting his thumb.

"But, Henry . . ."

There is a knock on the door. Four fingers slip around the corner as the door opens a crack. My mother's voice asks, "Are you boys hungry?"

Henry takes his thumb out of his mouth. He stands up. "Yes, thank you, Mrs. Schoen." It might be the light, but Henry appears to be reddening in those small patches of his face that are hairless.

"What would you like?"

Through the open door comes a strong waft of brownie-perfume. "Brownies would be fine, Ma," I say. She nods and goes back to the kitchen. This gives her two interruptions for the price of one.

Henry seems especially pleased with my mother today. "David, your mother is too much!"

I go over to the cabinets to return the Stones and to locate a tape of something by Berlioz. Henry's monologue begins to get to me, and I find myself threading the tape awkwardly. "So did you come to a final decision?"

"Oh yes, yes."

"Well how about letting the world know? I'm interested."

"I had all those catalogs — Harvard, Princeton, Stanford, Oxford, Reed, U.S.C., Hamilton, U.C.L.A., Wisconsin, Brown . . ." One for each finger.

"Which one did you pick?"

"I didn't pick any of them."

"Why not? They're all great."

Henry stands up. He crosses the room slowly. "No, they're not. I'm looking for revolutionary things: new courses, new ideas, new viewpoints. They all fall down somewhere."

"Even Harvard and Stanford?"

"Especially those two."

"But Henry, how can you judge a school by its catalog?"

"You can spot certain things. At first, Wisconsin appealed to me a great deal because it has a terrific African Studies program. But on second look, most of the courses are on the graduate level, and somewhere in the catalog it states that their aim is to train you 'to earn a living in a socially useful manner.' Now who needs that? I don't necessarily have to earn a living, or even be socially useful."

"Henry! Look, man, face facts. You're a middle-class kid. If you weren't middle-class, you wouldn't have to go to college. But I do see your point. That's kind of an irrelevant attitude for a university to have toward education."

"Brown was the most interesting — until I read their foreword. I always read that last. It states that one of Brown's educational aims is 'the refinement of emotional responses.' How can any post-Freudian scholar . . ."

"Yeah, you're right, you're right. But you're taking these catalogs too seriously. They mean nothing."

"Then why do they bother to put them out?"

"Supposedly, to help kids like us to make a decision. Besides, most people go by what they've heard."

"I know. In the end, that's what clinched this whole thing for me. My confusion is — or was — a result of the failure of these colleges to communicate. The medium is the message. They put out a thick, unreadable catalog full of faculty names, with lists of letters strung along after them — and those pages of calendars! Are they all so uptight that everything on that calendar must occur? Why can't they just print the date they open and let everything fall into place after that? They even have graduation day picked out. Supposing it rains? Suppose nobody wants to graduate? I mean, do they think all that nonsense is useful information? How do I know that they won't do the same in their courses? I'll end up learning things I don't want or need!" He pauses to sing a quotation from "Satisfaction" — . . . useless information, bum, ba, bum." Then he continues, "Princeton, David, says it has an interdenominational chapel to which they only invite Christian speakers. What about Muslim, Shinto, Zen, Hindu, *Jewish* — for God's sake — speakers! Which reminds me — this is funny, almost — in Brown's catalog they refer to Martin Buber as 'the Jewish thinker.' *I'm* Jewish, David. *You're* Jewish. *We* think. But we're not Martin Bubers." Enraged to the core, he has been shouting and stomping around in a circle.

I feel compelled to calm him, as he might inadvertently shake loose a delicate wire in a speaker or something. "It was just an unfortunate faux pas, Henry. Some dumb girl in the publications office probably wrote it and thought she sounded smart until some-

11

body fired her." This has the desired soothing effect.

Luckily my mother appears at the door, mysteriously beamed in from the kitchen, pitcher of cider in her right hand and plate of brownies in her left hand. Justice, truth, and beauty all wrapped up in one pink Swirl.

I go over and unburden her. "Thanks a lot, Ma. They look great. Hey, Henry, they're still hot!" I put the goodies down on the top of my desk, which, except for *The Life and Works of Sigmund Freud*, is stark clean. Standing, Henry hovers over the brownies to attack them one by one. I excuse myself for a moment to get three glasses from the kitchen. When I come back I find that Mother and Henry have been talking about Henry's college problems.

My mother is asking him, "So, Henry, you've made your choice, haven't you?" I hold my breath.

"Yes, Mrs. Schoen." Henry looks her right in the eyes.

My mother is standing very straight, like a scout-master. "What will it be?"

"Oberlin."

"Oberlin!" I protest. "No, no, man. I was sure you were going to pick Harvard. Oh, Henry. Why couldn't you at least have picked a school in New England?"

"Oberlin is a great school, Dave. Why should I go to school in New England?" Henry asks benignantly.

My mother's face stares in surprise. "Didn't David tell you? He was accepted by M.I.T. on early admissions. The letter came yesterday."

"David, that's incredible!" Henry does a love dance to the last strains of the symphony. "Yahoo!! Holy Mass-a-chu-setts In-sti-tute of Tech-nol-o-gee! Out of sight! Wow! Et cetera, et cetera, et cetera!"

Yesterday my parents very calmly received the news of my acceptance ("Well done, son, but your mother and I knew all along that you were going to get in"). The only extraordinary thing that happened was that my father kissed me, quickly — probably for the last time in my life — and my mother shook my hand. Now here is Henry spontaneously giving me the rites of passage that these small victories deserve. I look at Henry and ask, "Why Oberlin?"

Henry stops his raucous cavorting short. Berlioz has quit and the room is silent. Henry swallows. "The reason I'm going to Oberlin is that it has a long history of liberal education. It was the first to open its enrollment to all races, and the first to grant a B.A. to women. And they have the finest school of music in America."

"Are you going to study music, Henry?" my mother asks, smiling her special Mona Lisa I-know-what-you're-going-to-do-before-you-do-it smile.

"No, ma'am." Henry glances at the door. "But you see, this girl I met at the library yesterday — Sally — well, her father is a professor there, and they live there, and she says that . . ."

My mother and I look at each other. I start to laugh. She starts to laugh. I fold up on the bed. She slips to the floor, like butter melting in a fry pan. We are weak from laughter. Tears are streaming down my mother's cheeks. I am pounding the pillows with one arm, holding my sides with the other. We look up at sober Henry. All at once, he starts to laugh, too. So we three all laugh, stunned, until we think that we'll probably never, ever want to laugh again.

2

I AM SITTING on the floor of my room surrounded by papers, notebooks, old erasers, carbon paper, a broken tie clip, several buttons, spare spools for the tape recorder, pens that have run out of ink but which I was saving because I was going to buy refills for them, letters, postcards, newspaper clippings, a ring I got in a box of cereal a long time ago, rubber bands.

It is the day after the day after Labor Day. The most depressing day of the year. Yesterday I spent the day feeling tired and sunburnt and a little hung over, but today I'm just beginning to get nervous about going to school on Saturday; and, of course, the weather is hot and sticky and the air conditioner is going full blast, and so on top of being nervous I am also clammy. My mother told me to clean out my drawers and to give away clothing and things that I don't need anymore. It's hard to do, I find, because some things that you don't need, you need anyway. Take for example these three decks of cards. I could give away one pack, but suppose I lost one deck? How could my brother and I and our cousins tolerate each other when my aunts and uncles come here and we cousins are forced upon each other unless we can play canasta to pass the time? The third deck is insurance.

And these rubber bands. You *always* need rubber bands.

I fill two cartons with stuff to throw away. I still have another drawer to go through. I dump this one on top of the heap and paw through it, too. This drawer contains interesting things. The envelope and information it once contained about M.I.T. — preregistration, suitable courses for my major (psychology), a map of the school, forms, forms, and more forms. Luckily I got through all of that. I wonder if I should keep the remnants.

There are my salary stubs. Henry was right. We did sock away a lot of bread this summer. I have about $700 in my own account. I think he has about the same — maybe more because he did some extra work on the weekends. Back in the spring we were discussing whether or not we should get regular jobs this summer. See, for three summers in a row Henry has worked for free on one of the local papers and I've taken some kind of summer course. One year it was German, another it was driver's ed. Last summer I enrolled in an advanced math class. But this year, with college expenses looming up ahead of us, we both agreed that having money of our own would be a nice thing for both our parents and ourselves. Since we're always hanging around music stores and record shops and since the only thing we know well with any commercial value is music, we decided to keep asking until we found jobs. And of course the stores had to be air-conditioned. We weren't expecting to get jobs in the same place, but we did manage to get ones near each other. I worked at Sam Goody's and Henry worked at The Record Hunter. Not bad.

I worked partly on commission. Henry worked straight salary, which is just as well. Henry doesn't exactly like to hustle people. We came out even. Unfortunately my salesman's discount was too tempting. I spent about $100 on tapes and new records. Henry's sales resistance was a bit higher than mine. Besides, already having acquired everything made by the Stones, Henry is not really interested in possessing anything else.

Ten salary checks. Ten weeks. Where did they go? I remember a few days before school let out that we were cutting classes and going out to the Rockaways for some sun. Then there were a few days when it rained, after exams and graduation and everything were over with. And then we went to work. We met every morning on the subway platform. Henry lives

17

closer to another stop, but he'd walk over to meet me here so that we could have each other's company for that squeeze into downtown Manhattan. That first week was impossible. We'd just drag ourselves home and go to sleep. We didn't really revive until the beginning of the third week. Had enough strength to take a couple of chicks out, even. Went to a concert in Central Park. Fourth week. That's a blank. Fifth week — ah, yes, Arlo Guthrie came into the store one day that week. Somewhere in the seventh or eighth week we went up to Newport for the festival. Although — well, I was going to compare it to Woodstock. No use. Then this weekend out at Montauk Point — huge party, lots of beer, friends, hamburgers, sand. Everybody all psyched to go to school. Happens every year, anyway, even when it's not college and all that means. Summer just gets to be a drag around August. I've never not wanted to go back to school. Never. Even during the winter, when the excitement has worn off, I still dig books and the people there and the challenge of tests, papers, projects. Henry says I'm queer on school. He's queer on extracurricular stuff: writing, journalism club, the above- as well as the underground papers — things like that. Well, I like school, don't know exactly why yet, but I do. And here it comes on Saturday. School with a capital S. College. The axis around which my days in high school have pivoted. The magnet at the end of four years' worth of study.

There are some movie stubs. The Elgin. Some old Bogart film we went to one weekend. Not *Casablanca*

. . . something else. Can't remember. Seems like a hundred years ago.

A newspaper clipping. I put it here a year ago . . . maybe more . . . I was going to give it to Henry. It says:

COUPLE DIE IN PARKED CAR
MONOXIDE KILLS YOUTH AND GIRL
from the *Blade* correspondent

Athena, O. Rex R. Royce, 19, of Athena, and a companion, Rosemary Kline, 16, of Elysia, died Wednesday night of carbon monoxide poisoning while parked in a car on Pickle Road near here.

Fred Bird, Wood County sheriff's deputy, said that he discovered the teen-agers about 9:30 P.M. The car's engine was running and the windows were closed.

Dr. William Duke, Wood County coroner, ruled the death accidental due to carbon monoxide poisoning . . .

I am surprised to find this clipping. I thought it had disappeared. I was going to give it to Henry. Yes — because I thought that he might make a story out of it. Forgot all about it. Still wonder what they were doing in that car. Making it?

And here is an envelope containing the clipped-out article on Rollo May that I found last spring in the *New York Times*. How I admire men like him. Of course my first idol is Freud. Not so much for his findings, but for *beginning*. For defying his social circle. I don't understand everything he wrote, but I've read it all. Every book and article that I could get my hands on. I've also read Adler and Jung and Erikson and biographies of them all.

I'll be a psychologist one day. I want to study human behavior and all the facets of the mind. I won't have an office filled with housewives and homosexuals. No. I'm going to have a lab. I'll do clinical tests and studies of normal behavior. I want to see what the limits are — if there are any — to human potential. Maybe I'll uncover a key to the prevention of mental retardation . . . It's a fantastic picture in my mind. Me in a long white coat surrounded by lab assistants and notebooks, encased in equipment and one-way glass, the sounds of animals in the background. Maybe I'll teach. I'll definitely publish. There I am in my house. My study. One shelf is filled with my own books. One wall of the room is smoked glass. The other three are just books. A pipe rack on the wall. Something tall and green growing in a corner pot. A small stone sculpture on the desk.

I put the article into a box containing the things I am saving. I stuff everything else in the throwaway box.

There are some small sheets of paper. Found poems! I found my lost found poems! So here's where they've been. One is called "Good-bye." It is appropriate for today. Today when I am throwing out all of my debris, all my extras. Perhaps after death there will be this scene where some celestial garbage man greets you at the Pearly Gates. "David, my boy," he'll say, sorting through the piles of garbage behind him, "you did a good job. You consumed six hundred cans of Campbell's tomato soup, seven thousand peanut butter and jelly sandwiches (here are the crusts), nine thousand rolls of toilet tissue, twelve cars, four houses, one thousand reams of paper, three hundred typewriter ribbons, six hundred seventeen light bulbs, nine thousand six hundred forty-five Q-tips, and seventy pounds of Jell-O. Not only that, but you wrote six thousand two hundred ninety-five letters (twenty of which were saved by your friends and loved ones) made six hundred thirteen long-distance phone calls, used up eleven million nine hundred eighty-nine thousand seven hundred eighty-seven kilowatts and five pairs of glasses."

I am almost finished with my throwing-out project. Before I start packing my clothes I read my poem — "found" in Roget's Thesaurus when I was supposed to be writing an English term paper.

Good-bye

separation;
parting &c. v.;

detachment, segregation;
divorce

sejunction, seposition, diduction,
diremption, discerption;

elision; caesura, division,
subdivision, break, fracture, rupture;

21

compartition; dis-
memberment, — inte-
gration, -location;

luxation; sever-,
dis-sever-ance;
scission; re —,
ab-scission;
circumcision;
lacer —
dilacer-ation;
dis-ab-ruption;

avulsion; divulsion;
section, resection, cleavage;
fision; separability;
separatism.

fissure, breach, rent,
split, rift, crack,
slit, slot, incision.

dissection, anatomy;
decomposition &c. 49

Good-bye. Good-bye high school, New York City,
temperature-humidity inversions, parents, television,
bed, old friends — except Henry, of course.

Hello, Saturday. Hello M.I.T. Hello, hello, hello.

Part II

1

"HELLO, DAVID . . . ?" Henry is 800 miles away and his voice crackles over the phone. "What took you so long?"

"I was in the john. You're out of your mind to call."

"Yeah, but I just wanted to talk. Some guy told me there's something wrong with this phone — broken, or something — and that you can call any place in the world for free."

"Hope he's right," I say, feeling nervous. "You could call me every week and then I won't have to write letters all the time."

"Hey, yeah." Henry blows his nose. "Isn't this freshman nonsense ridiculous?"

25

"It's not so bad. What have you been doing?"

"Sneezing a lot. They must cultivate pollen here on the farms. I may be the first hay-fever mortality the world has ever known." Henry does sound a bit clogged up.

"Have you been filling out forms and running to meetings?"

"Not too many forms. I counted them. There were five for registration, six file cards, some kind of personality profile, a language placement test, and an advanced-placement English test."

"But you'd taken those tests."

"No, man. I took Princeton's little computer test that everyone else takes. Here you have to take *their* test. They're tricky people, here." Henry blows his nose again.

"Everything we had to fill out was on computer cards. Sort of freaky spending hours filling out little dots and squares."

"What are you taking?" Henry makes some noise — like he's yawning.

"Psych, chem, calculus, German, and comparative literature."

"Heavy. Heav-y."

"What about you?"

There are three or four sneezes, then a silence, then two more. "Oh, man. This is terrible. Can't talk too long. I only have three more tissues left."

"What are you taking, man?"

"Oh, yeah. When I got here I got this note from a dean and I went to see him. He said that maybe I ought to take a special program. It's experimental and its supposed to be flexible and, you know, 'creative.' I hear that the younger faculty is teaching it, and that for the writing seminar there's a novelist and a poet sharing the course. But I've never heard of them."

"Oh. Well."

"So, what else am I taking . . . History of Social Protest, this writers' workshop, a reading course in non-Western literatures, a philosophy course called Exploration — this semester is on student values versus ancient Greek philosophy. There are other parts to this course next semester. Oh, and I'm taking Creative Movement."

"What the hell is Creative Movement?" My voice must sound a little shrill.

"It's, ah . . ."

A noise stops him. "Please signal when through."

"Is this the operator?" Henry wheezes, which he tends to do anyway, but his hay fever has made him sound like a calliope.

"Yes, it is. Your three minutes are up. Please signal . . ."

"O.K., O.K." She clicks off. "Jesus Christ." Henry's voice is getting asthmatic, his breathing sounds like chocolate pudding. There are thudding noises. "Shit." The muffled thuds continue. I am hoping that the operator is not listening to the curses coming from both ends of the conversation. From long experience with Henry, I can identify the thuds as the sounds made by his hairy head smashing rhythmically, fetus-like, against the steel uterus of the phone booth.

I can almost see the perspiration beading on his forehead, wetting his nose, and causing his wire-rimmed glasses to slip down, his red-plaid flannel shirt dampening along his broad back. "Oh, shit."

"You're being redundant." I am perspiring a bit myself.

"But David, I have something that might take hours to discuss. It's urgent. You have to help me."

"A girl?"

"No," he says emphatically.

"Well, then how urgent could it be?"

"David . . ."

"Write me a letter. This is going to cost money."

"I know. I know. But you have to promise to write."

"Yeah, I will. I promise. Now, we've got to bolt. You write first. Good-bye." I put down the phone and walk quickly down the hall to the first staircase. I go up a flight. Then I walk down the next staircase, and back down the corridor. Only I must have done something wrong because I am all twisted around. I walk around for about half an hour before I finally find my room. The only thing that makes the situation even mildly amusing is the thought of Henry struggling to free himself from the embrace of the phone booth. Extracting himself from small places is one of Henry's problems, along with a lack of invisibility.

Now, as for myself, I look pretty much like anybody else: brown hair — not too long, not too short — dark-rimmed glasses, skinny. But Henry, well,

Henry always manages to be in the spotlight. He's heavy and awkward; his feet knock into his ankles when he walks along studying the sidewalk. And then, of course, his face is almost obliterated by curling masses of hair. So for Henry to slip off into the dusk of a remote corner of the dorm would be impossible. In fact, when I get back to my room I laugh because I have to think that maybe Henry never made it out of the booth at all.

I don't bother to explain what has happened to my roommate Ted, because he's busy rapping with some guy from Nashville about Country and Western music about which I know from nothing. So I listen for a while before turning in. Before falling asleep, I think how Henry's conscience must be bothering him about the call, about how he's always called the phone company a monopolistic oppressor, about how he's going to have to wrestle with his monumental Problem, whatever that is, alone, because I'm very bad in the advice department although I am curious to know what the Problem could possibly be. Then my mind's eye returns to the phone booth and Henry trapped inside with the phone shrieking in his ear. I think I begin to dream about it. I can only be sure of thinking one thing: whatever Creative Movement is, Henry needs it.

2

Two, MAYBE THREE DAYS LATER, I get a long fat envelope in the mail. The address is sort of smeary, and from the Scotch tape wrinkling across the back of the envelope, it's obvious that it had been sealed and then opened and then resealed. Such ambivalence could only be Henry's. I am walking to lunch with my roommate, Ted, who does not talk very much when he's hungry. In fact, Ted is not inclined to talk very much at all. We have sort of a typical new-room-mate relationship: kind of mutually dependent, yet a little distant. Sort of friendship by default. The kind of thing that might happen in a fallout shelter. We don't know very much about each other, but I sus-

30

pect that Ted doesn't really like being in school. Like maybe he should have gone into VISTA or worked for a while. He's from a minuscule coastal town in Maine where everybody knows him. Here he's lost. There are just too many things to do, too many faces and streets. You can tell he's on edge most of the time. Sometimes he whistles tunelessly to himself, which to me is as annoying as fingernails on a blackboard would be to someone else. But I don't want to say anything to him about it yet. That's what I mean about our relationship. It's a little too polite, right now. But then again, I probably do something that bugs him. He'll tell me in time, I suppose, and then I'll tell him about his whistling.

"Your letter," Ted says, glancing at the envelope, "who's it from?"

"It's from this guy I went to high school with," I say.

It feels odd to refer to Henry in such vague terms. Henry is so real to me. Not like other people, you know, who are faces and words and who do certain things for you or with you but whom you never quite figure out. I mean, it's like the difference between a painting and a sculpture. Henry is very real. I can see him and touch him. Other people — no, they're all kind of vague. I can't walk around them and describe them. What's more, I can't tell what they think about me. So I feel a bit guilty saying this vague thing to Ted about Henry.

After a short silence, Ted says, "Aren't you going to open it?"

"Oh, yeah. But it looks a bit long. I'll wait till we get to the dining hall."

"Umm." Ted is quiet for a moment. He shifts his books to his right hand. He puts his left hand in his pocket. "Haven't gotten any mail since I got here."

"What do you mean?" I say. "You got a letter from your parents yesterday."

"Uh, yeah. But they don't count." Ted laughs.

"You mean, unless they enclose a little something inside."

"Right."

We get on line. The hall is crowded. The air is filled with smoke and talk and the clink of cheap stainless steel against heavy porcelain. We put an assortment of foods on our green plastic trays: some kind of grade Z steak sandwich oozing with brown-colored gravy and droopy onions, also several colors of Jell-O and about a pound of bread and butter each. We find a table with a couple of empty places and we sit down, tossing our books loudly on the floor beside us. After sawing through the steak, I begin to open the letter. I peek in.

"That's a relief," I say.

"What is?" Ted asks.

"Most of this is clippings and stuff. The letter is only a couple of pages." I glance at the handwritten sheets. "Good thing I'm an amateur cryptologist. Henry writes in Linear B."

"Terrific," Ted comments, pretending that what he is drinking is coffee.

I proceed.

32

"David," it begins, "I was just sitting there, under one of those proverbial spreading chestnut trees on the campus (Pray, am I the Village Smithie, with arms like iron butterflies? No, I am too far from Northampton, Mass.), and I decided (dah-dah!) that of all the people I know, you most personify squirrel-ness. Diligence is your middle name. (David Diligence Schoen.) In fact, I'll bet that it's hard for someone who is watching you (the FBI, Army Intelligence, your mother) to tell whether you are playing or are doing something constructive. So I would suppose they look at your record: marks, deportment, attendance, and conclude that surely you must be industrious. However, in my opinion you are just scurrying around, giving the illusion of being a squirrel — er, student. Take, for example, Milton. Not the poet. The squirrel in the chestnut tree under which I was spreading. Now, Milton has a heart of gold, and I'm sure it wasn't anything personal (squirrels aren't anti-Semitic, are they?), but all the time I was there under the tree trying desperately to take a nap, he kept blitzing me with twigs and shells and stuff. Annoying, what? And so I folded myself up like an Arab and quietly ran to the library, whose hallowed halls are this moment inspiring me with their 100 years of dust and academic freedom to write this letter to you this day.

"Aside from the fact that I got caught the other night, it was nice talking with you. The operator started to ring back about nine milliseconds after we hung up. I flew into a panicked rage, and when the door finally unstuck and I regained my senses, I zoomed down the hall to the men's room where I thought I could at least hide, not to mention take care of some of nature's crass bodily functions. Unfortunately something called an Albert Jerome Faberman, Jr., came ambling down the hall hand in hand with his enormous Super-Ego (to compensate for having been deprived of a personality, no doubt) and picked up the phone. Not only that, but he told the operator my name (how he even knows me, I can't figure . . .) and address. And then, as if this was not enough, he trotted down the hall to the john and told me of his perfidity. Being committed to non-violence, I merely insulted his mother, his father, his questionable masculinity, and the like. He almost cried. But how, I ask you, can a kid like that exist? Could he have sprung, whole, a college freshman, from the head of an AT&T computer? Oh, well, what's $10, I always say.

"Anyway, after the fracas, I was so upset that I sort of collided with this incredible guy, a senior, and his equally incredible chick (only I shouldn't say chick because she's into Women's Lib and would resent that kind of dirty talk) on their way out to have a dinner of cheese and bread and fruit under the stars and the moon. Since they had enough food for about ten people, they were trying to recruit some freshmen — it was their idea of charity work. When I volunteered to buy the wine — that is, pay for it: in this provincial wasteland you have to be 21 to buy wine! — they decided to abandon their hunt and split for the woods.

34

They found me a girl so that the beast in my soul would be quelled, I suppose, à la *Women in Love* or something like that. This girl . . . well, she wasn't so bad, but she was a little put off, so to speak. Probably because she's a senior and I am a lowly, lowly freshman. All the time I kept getting the feeling that she was about to ask me if I had gone through puberty yet. She has her hang-ups, I've got mine.

"I dug the other two, though. He's studying music history and she's a cellist. Their names are Silvana and Paul and they hadn't ever tried Almadén wines before. Their tastes, they said, ran to the expensive imports. They learned, though. They've been around quite a bit. They've been together for two years and they spent the summer together in Europe. Hence the expensive taste. They're really beautiful together. Except that maybe a whole summer was too confining, emotionally. Like, she says she wants to play for an orchestra and he says he wants to be a musicologist, but I think what's going on underneath a lot of their talk is that he wants to marry her and she doesn't want marriage at all. I wonder what it would be like traveling around, living with a girl. Much different from sweaty little evenings at the drive-in, not that I've ever had much of that. This other girl, Betty, she kind of frightens me. Even though she looks as though she eats apple pie for breakfast. Maybe she didn't like me because I kept to my side of the loaf of bread all night, despite the jug of wine and the bough.

"I'm also having trouble getting used to these apolitical self-interested creative types I find here. People may think I talk funny, but man, these sensitive souls are very serious about themselves. Take Silvana. Every day that they were in Europe, she would practice for four hours. (She said it was easy in Spain and Italy: there was nothing else to do during siesta . . .) But people would hear her playing in the parks and hotel lobbies and things, and they would invite them both to appear at parties and dinners. So she and Paul went to all these incredible fat-city functions and performed for the industrialists and élite while strikes and governmental crises and pollution gripped the Continent. Even as students, they continue to be sort of above everything. (You *do* know how that is, David, don't you?)

"I could tell you more about them, but I haven't gotten to my Problem, yet, and I think I'd better before it comes time to go to dinner. (They serve really good food here.) The problem is my roommate. Classical, isn't it? After five days, I know I just can't make it through a month with him, much less the whole year. I don't know how they threw us together . . . one of those cards may have been spindled when it went through the Univac. He's unbelievably weird. A veritable Blifil. First off, instead of being competitive, he's motivated by pure unadulterated jealousy. Plus he talks through his nose and has pimples. In front of my *parents*, mind you, while my mother is unpacking my sweaters and my father is pretending he's not really going to cry, he had the balls to ask me, "You're not really a Merit Scholar, are you?" (I guess somewhere there was something posted about the freshmen who had entered with awards and special prizes . . .) I was stunned, but my parents were enraged. You know how they feel about these things. So my mother, in her best Bella Abzug style, told him off, calling him a little twerp. It was cool. I was grateful that his parents had already left, otherwise it could have turned into a Scene. Anyway, so now Twerp has gotten the idea that he's going to get better marks than me. Thank God he's in none of my seminars. But he's still going to try to outdo me in points. He'll probably jam my typewriter or burn my notes. I suppose if I weren't living with him, I could laugh at him. He's neat, he's clean, he sharpens his pencils (which have his name stamped on them, like he was in third grade!) before he goes to bed, and polishes his shoes every night at 10:15. But, the coup de grâce to my self-image as a New Yorker Who Has Seen Every Thing and Every Body is that this kid gets into bed, hauls out a *huge* family-type Bible, and meditates for 5 minutes every night. Can you imagine! An eighteen-year-old kid in this day and age trying to embarrass another kid . . . after all, there are private chapels (and smaller Bibles) on campus. And I think I'll beat him up if he ever says anything about going to church or praying with him or repenting my sins. God knows that I've sinned few enough times, anyway . . . I talked to the dorm adviser yesterday, and he said that unless there's a stronger excuse, I can't move out on him because there's really no place for me to go at the moment. But he said if I really can't get my work done, that it could all be worked out. But you must have some suggestions. What can I possibly do? Please write back as quick as you can . . . Henry.

"P.S. Have seen my old friend Sally, the professor's daughter, a couple of times. I still like her, but more as a friend: a very pretty friend, I admit. Though I might just be intimidated now that I'm here and it looks like I'll be taking her dad's course next term. He's one of the best, they say."

The envelope is filled with other things. Clippings, mimeographed notices, cartoons. I glance at them briefly before stuffing them back. I notice the time. "Aha, the little hand is on the one and the big hand is almost on the six." Papers begin to shuffle, plates and trays collide. "Lab time."

"Henry sounds cool," Ted says, smiling.

"Yes, indeed. Henry is a character, though. A good friend, very smart, but a character, nevertheless. For instance, this girl, Sally . . . well, he sort of bumped into her on Fifth Avenue last year. That's the way Henry meets everybody. He manages to be both very clumsy and very sensitive to personal magnetism. It has led to some delicate encounters, but usually he winds up with more friends. So, the day he met Sally was when he had started to lose his mind over college admissions. See, Henry's problem then was the obverse of everyone else's, which is that he knew that he'd get into any place he applied. This unlimited scope tends to confuse people, you see."

"I see," Ted interjects.

"Yes, well, so after he met this girl and found out that Daddy was a professor and that she was going to be there, out in the wilds of Ohio, and also that it was a good school and one he hadn't thought of but should have, well, then he decided to go there."

"You mean, just because of her? He was in love with her?"

"Oh, no. You don't understand Henry. You see, what he needed was for his father or a guidance counselor or me, maybe, to say, 'Henry, you are going to go to such and such,' and he would have gone. But everybody just kept suggesting more and more places to him, and more and more specialized majors. And nobody really understood what he was going through. So eventually he met Sally, who in addition to being very pretty, is also smart and utterly sincere. Anyway, so she must have said to him, 'Why don't you go to Oberlin, where Daddy teaches?' Well, whatever she said, she resolved the question and Henry was able to function as a normal human being. Also, she was his first girl, in a platonic sort of way."

Ted's eyebrows rise. "But he's not in love with her?"

"In love?" I repeat, casually. "Henry? You just don't know Henry. He's not very good with girls," I say, much too confidently.

3

THE NEXT LETTER I get from Henry comes a week later. It is airmail, special delivery. This makes me feel guilty because I haven't written him back. The week has just been too much. Books to read, labs, and all the news. The news was that there were a lot of bombings all around the country. Out in the sticks. A couple of cops get shot, a few bombings — banks and such. Big state universities are preparing for the Big Siege: hiring munitions-demolition experts and security guards instead of English professors.

I kept wishing last week that it would all go away; I had enough to worry about without the Revolution.

It was just that every time I turned around it seemed that Ted was clipping some article out of the *Globe* or the *Times*, or tacking up a new anti-establishment poster. Around Wednesday I started thinking that this new-roommate politeness was not helping . . . that maybe it was time to start thinking of asking him to cool it. But nothing I could think of saying sounded right. It kept coming out sort of bitchy. Could I have said, "Those posters don't prove anything"? Or "Couldn't you be a revolutionary without advertising it?" Or "Do you have to cut up my *Times*?" (which was actually what was bugging me the most)?

There it is, every day, my precious *Times* for which I have to pay an exorbitant amount of money, shredded, bowdlerized, disemboweled. Also, the room will never quite look the same, what with little bits of paper accumulating under the beds and on the windowsills. And since Ted has no classes the hour the paper arrives, he picks it up and performs surgery before I even get a peek at the headlines. This is what truly enrages me to my very bones. But this is my own hang-up. It probably comes from having an older brother who would snatch anything from me and read and/or eat it first. Probably many middle-class children come to know the pangs of poverty in the same way: by being somebody's younger sibling. I would even suspect that you won't catch first sons and daughters at poverty-program meetings and the like. Antipoverty workers must surely all be younger sisters and brothers.

41

Thus, I did a slow burn all week long. There was a chemistry quiz on Thursday, and I was determined to concentrate on that. Once that was over, with the sense of liberation intoxicating me into forgetting the other little quizzes coming up on Tuesday in math and German, I went with Ted to hear a speaker Thursday night. Ted looked determined to go, and somehow his eagerness made me more curious. He hadn't seemed very interested in much lately besides making paper pollution in the room.

The Union was crowded when we got there. We sat on the floor. The speaker came out. He looked more like an old kid than a clever and experienced lawyer. His suit was somewhat rumpled. He wore a broad bold tie. His hands were large and bony, and he frequently ran his fingers through his thinning blond hair. His voice was strong and to us he seemed sympathetic and dynamic. We were transfixed with a clammy fear as he told of the unconstitutionality of many of the laws being enacted, of the political motivation behind foreign policy positions, of the history of the Vietnam war. He cited the consequences of certain new laws, the reform bills that congress had been unable to pass because of lack of money or the President's veto. And he described McCarthyism in tragic detail. He assured us that students would now be expected to conform or else they would be blackmailed or bullied into silence. Statements were already being made by legislators that campus unrest had cost so many millions of dollars that the taxpayer was "at long last" refusing to foot the bill. He cli-

maxed by naming the chain of command from the
state assembly on down, which had pressured the
student governing body to cancel his speaking en-
gagement here. He knew *how* to speak, which was
nine tenths of the problem. A radical Spiro Agnew,
someone called him. It was effective, though. Afterward I felt confused, angry, skeptical. It was very hard
to believe these things. One nation under God, and
all that.

Ted was silent on the way back to the dorm. All
around us guys were saying: "He's right, he's right"
"We must face oppression and defeat it" "All power
to the people" "Right on . . ." Ted and I argued
quite a bit that night about it. He called me a fence
sitter and quoted me from Mao whose Little-Read
Book (as I call it) he now reads in bed every night
— like Henry's roommate and the Bible. (Jesus!) Ted
seemed sort of exhilarated by this speech. It was a
bore. It's all been said, so many times. But Ted still
thinks it is something brand-new. I think it frightens
him, but he eats it up anyway.

Being at school these days — any school, I guess —
is like standing on Lexington Avenue uptown during
the rush hour. Everything is going on at once. People
cascade from their office buildings and out onto the
street. They flee home. But you might be standing
there on the corner, the way I did last summer many
times waiting for Henry to meet me, and you might
suddenly, amidst the noise and confusion of the
crowds, feel the faint tremor of the subway lurching

43

beneath your tired feet. After a while you might not even bother to think about it, but you know, in some deep corner of your head, that there's a whole city of motion speeding invisibly beneath you. What I mean is, no matter where you go to school, and no matter what you see or think you see going on around you, there's always *something* happening that, well, maybe you don't choose to see but you know is there. Do you see what I mean?

So now I have Henry's second letter in my hand. Feeling guilty, I have to justify why I haven't written. I tell myself that when one has chem and math and German quizzes to deal with, plus a roommate running around with my *New York Times* in one hand and *Quotations from Chairman Mao* in the other, well, then one really has some good excuses for not writing. This all goes through my mind before I find it in myself to dare to open the letter. This time it really is a tome. I decide not to read it there and trudge back to the dorm. I try to imagine what he wrote. I think maybe I ought to open it up and read it on the way, but it is drizzling. In only a couple of weeks here, I have discovered that life in Massachusetts is an unending precipitation. In all seasons something is falling out of the sky. On me. So I decide not to read the epistle.

I have to think back to Queens. I wonder what Ted would have made of Henry then. Then? Last year, though it seems like another lifetime. Henry, and me, too, I guess, were into the kind of revolutionary rhetoric that Ted is having his first exposure to.

That's why it all kind of bounces off me. Henry's cooled off somewhat in the political sphere, but I guess his personality will always remain that of the ultimate nonconformist. I decide to tell Henry about Ted. Henry's an intelligent listener. And he, of all people, would understand Ted's schtick. Last year he was writing editorials (anonymous, of course) for an underground paper in Brooklyn. They were very good. Unlike Henry's usual projects, it wasn't purely aesthetic. It was political, but at the time Henry insisted that he had founded a new "aesthetics of politics." It kept him busy for a while and then suddenly he dropped it. No more Marcuse, no more People's Revolution. The silence, as they say, was deafening. At first I thought, Terrific, he's disenchanted with the movement (like me), and then paranoid old me started to think that maybe he was hiding something. But Henry isn't complicated enough to have intellectual allegiance to one philosophy and to express a more moderate viewpoint in public. So I put it to him, in a vague kind of way, and his reply was, "You know who the People are, David? The People are hard-hats and Wall Street secretaries and truck drivers and farmers. I don't think these people are going to revolt, because they are basically anti-intellectual in this country. History has taught them not to trust us because we always cop out on them. Look at Martin Luther and the Peasants' Revolt . . ." And so on, into the night.

When I get back to the room, I shove things aside and make some kind of room on the bed. I am sur-

prised and relieved that the letter is typed. I can't
type and I guess I had assumed that Henry couldn't
either. But I had forgotten all those newspapers he
wrote for and all those rejected stories sent to *The
New Yorker* and the like. Guess he had to learn.

"David . . . I am typing this because something
incredible happened this week, which seems so far
out that it actually seems like a story or something,
so I'm going to have to tell it like a story, very com-
plete, so that I can somehow understand what's going
on. Believe me, I'm not telling you this out of chau-
vinism but confusion, and I hope that by telling you
who understands me so well, that it will become more
'real' to me.

"Remember I told you about meeting Silvana and
Paul and Betty, the snobby blond who didn't like me,
and how we all went out with some wine and cheese
and bread into the woods and had a moonlight sup-
per? Well, when I went to my first Creative Movement class two days later, it turned out that Betty
takes it too. She's not at all bad-looking — especially
in dance tights — just a bit intimidating, at first. The
guys have to wear tights, too, which embarrassed the
hell out of me. They're very . . . well . . . tight and
you know what a grotesque body I have, but Betty
said later that it's my self-image that's grotesque.
She says the old bod is O.K. I'm supposed to try to
stand up straight, though. *Her* body is so beautiful
in motion. She has such control over it. When I
think how I've been treating my body, I feel terrible.

46

I mean, about all it does is provide transportation for my head. This class will help. (So will Betty . . .)

"I ran into her right outside the men's locker room. I was with another guy and we were joking around, you know, taking leaps and stuff, pretending to be Rudi Nureyevs, only getting about 2″ above the ground instead of 6′. Betty came along, slim and cool, all in tight black, like black-cotton paint smoothed along her skin. A Negro with white hands and feet and face. She and I said hello and we walked into the dance studio together. I don't remember what happened to the guy I had been with. I was nervous and I told her how stupid I thought I looked. She was reassuring, saying it would take a while to get 'physically oriented' to myself and that she thought this class was perfect for improving that. Which was why she liked this particular course and kept taking it over every semester. It's the same, she said, but somehow different each time. Like love, she said.

"The course is supposed to teach you to first of all relate your body to space, and second, to relate spatial movement to the other arts, such as music and painting and poetry. It's not supposed to require any skills in dancing, but it's not easy and the instructor keeps emphasizing concentration. Yoga, anyone? We exercised to warm up, and then we were told to form couples. Naturally I ran over to Betty. We were told to make igloos around ourselves by sitting on the floor and pressing outward with our flattened palms, as high and round as we would go without lifting our asses off the floor. After we did that, one of the partners was to stand outside the igloo and follow the other's hand as he traced the walls. So Betty would feel the outside and I would feel the inside. It became a very beautiful movement. My hand even began to feel a little cold. I found that this 'play' brought Betty and me together, psychically, like two little kids with the same retinue of imaginary friends.

"After class, I didn't see her. She may have stayed around for another dance class or to go for a swim. I didn't think about her until the next day at breakfast and then, oddly, just as I was remembering her face and her shoulders and the nice way her back met her legs, Betty herself appeared. She sat down and some other girls joined us. We talked for a few minutes and then we all had to run off to class. Around 4:00, on my way to the dorm, I ran into Betty again and so we had coffee and then went over to dinner together. Then I went to the library to do some research and she had to go to some meeting. Our dinner conversation was not particularly enlightening and she seemed like just a good-looking girl who was being maybe a little *too* kind — you know, in a condescending way.

"I didn't see her the next day, Friday, although when some guys and I were going to see an old Bergman film over at the Union, I thought I saw her walking with some tall guy . . . but it was dark and it could have been someone else. Saturday I got up late, rambled over to breakfast, picked up the *Plain Dealer*, and decided to feast myself on the rubbery French toast they serve for breakfast. I ate and read alone and then I went back to my room. My room-mate, luckily, was going to be gone for the weekend. So I shut the door and started to work on a paper for my Exploration seminar. About an hour later I heard a knock on the door. 'Come in,' I yelled, 'but you can only stay five minutes.' I was expecting one of the guys from down the hall — and you know how guys can hold you up when they just come in and park. But it was Betty. I never expected to be able to wheedle a girl into coming up to my room even during the day. You can imagine the shocked look on my face when I looked up from my desk to see Betty there.

" 'Can't I stay a little longer? Maybe six minutes?' She raised her eyebrows and her face seemed to open. She hadn't smiled so beautifully those other times.

" 'Absolutely not!' I said solemnly. But she had already closed the door behind her. She came close to where I was sitting, and leaning over the desk, she said, 'Hmmm, the man's busy.'

" 'Philosophizing,' I said, noticing that she wasn't wearing a bra under her knitted shirt. I tried to look up at her eyes which I just noticed were a lemony cinnamon, but I was distracted. The shirt was yellow and had buttons down the front. There were five buttons. The top and bottom ones were open. She also wore jeans. I was so confused that I barely heard what she was saying — something about what a lovely day it was and how she wanted to go for a walk and she guessed that I was too busy to go along. I'm not certain if that was really what she was saying, though.

49

I don't remember what I said or how long this quasi-conversation went on. I don't remember what I said, or if I said anything at all. Through a cloud or gauze like they did in *Romeo and Juliet* (or was it *Taming of the Shrew*? Zeffirelli, in any case). I watched her unbutton the second-from-the-bottom button on her shirt. I tried to look away, hoping something would pop into my mouth to say that wouldn't embarrass me. I found myself watching her in the mirror. At first she was sitting on the foot of the bed, and then she lay back, her blond hair just fanning out around her head with little curls. I couldn't look directly at her. I could see her unbutton another button. There was only one left. I was talking with her, I think. At least my mouth was moving. I walked over to the window and played with the shade pull. I heard her giggle. In the glare, I could see that she had undone the final button. A narrow strip of white skin shimmered between the yellow of the shirt. I *had* to turn around now. It was apparent that I had already been caught; the challenge was a little too blatant to ignore. Her cinnamon eyes were laughing at me. I sat down next to her, next to her head. She was upside down and her eyes didn't seem to laugh so much this way. I remember saying, 'Why do they call you Betty? That's my least favorite name in the whole world.'

" 'My real name is Elizabeth.'

" 'As in *Entertainment for Elizabeth*?'

" 'You're not very sweet.' She smiled wickedly. 'Why are you blushing?'

" 'I am not blushing.'

"She reached up to my face and tapped my cheek with her finger. As she stretched, one half of the yellow fell away; then she turned slightly and the other half fell away. I've never seen a girl's naked body before. Not a real girl. Not real skin. All the other times with girls it had been in the dark, in the cold chastity of Manhattan, through a dress, a bra, a slip. Never the real skin, the softness of real breasts so close to my hand. I was afraid, so I just touched her hair, her ears, her neck. Footsteps passed softly past my door. My head jerked up. She raised herself on one arm, the other still extended to my cheek. 'I locked it when I came in.' She smiled. Now she was facing me, and I had to see her eyes, her skin, yes, all of her skin. Her arms were around my neck. Sitting there, my heart pounding, I couldn't kiss her. She drew me close. I was on fire, and yet at the same time, afraid. I honestly don't know of what, but I was afraid. The loudest sound in the world was the ticking of the alarm clock. I looked at the ceiling. I kept thinking, But I don't even like her that much.

"Her eyes were Machiavellian, demanding, as it were, control over me, my body, my emotions. This was a bit much, from a girl I didn't especially dig. So I got up and walked out of the door. Zoom. Down the hall. Zoom. Out into the woods. Back in the closet was my jacket, and my glasses were still on my desk. I've never gone anywhere without my glasses before. Especially not outdoors. I was cold, too. But I had to walk around. Maybe half an hour later I came back, feeling rather dumb, thinking maybe there was something wrong with me. I mean, here's this chick taking off her clothes and everything, and I walk out. Still, the situation was a bit too Norman Mailer — like I felt as though I had already read about myself in a short story.

"I kept praying that she'd be gone when I got back to the room. She wasn't. She was curled up on the bed, asleep. When I shut the door she woke up. I sat down by the desk. She looked at me for a long time without saying anything. Then she looked down at the bedspread.

" 'I'm sorry,' she whispered.

" 'Me, too.' I didn't know what to say next. I thought maybe she would get up and leave. But she kept sitting there. 'Want to go for a hamburger?'

" 'Not especially,' " she said. More awkward silence. 'Look, I'm really sorry, Henry. I — I — I came in here uninvited and I interrupted your work and I insulted you . . .'

" 'I don't feel insulted,' I said, calmly.

" 'Yes, but, you know . . . And you behaved very sensibly. They used to call it like a gentleman, in quotes. And I feel, well, bad.' Her eyes were still lowered.

"I really was beginning to feel hungry and the smell of hamburger seemed to be there in the room. It was probably my sneakers. 'Are you sure you don't want a hamburger?'

" 'No.'

" 'Not even one with catsup and relish and onion

rings and Swiss cheese and a toasted bun and kosher pickle slices and greasy French fries on the side?'

" 'Do you know what I want?' She looked right at me. 'I want what happened before to not have happened. I realize that I jeopardized a potential relationship all in the name of ego. Before, I had thought you were cute in a kind of funny, awkward little freshman way and I thought, Wouldn't it be a laugh to see what this poor little guy would do in that situation? I mean, it would be a switch on the usual plot. Where the guys are trying to get into all the pants they can.'

" 'Would you have slept with me?' I asked out of curiosity.

" 'Yes, I think so.'

" 'Would you sleep with me some other time?'

" 'When?'

" 'When I want to. How should *I* know?'

" 'Maybe. Maybe. Yeah. I don't know. It would depend.'

" 'You're a bitch.' I was looking her straight in the eye. Angry, but smiling.

" 'I was waiting for that.' She smiled. 'Can we go for that hamburger now?'

"So David-i-doo, you *tell* me. You study psychology and behavioral sciences. You tell me. Why the hell did this all happen? In addition to this chick, I have good old Sally to worry about. She's not terribly eager to sleep with anyone, which is fine with me. Also I can't help thinking that her old man is going to be my professor next quarter. But I really, really dig her.

"Oh, and I solved the mystery of my roommate's nocturnal piety. Its object is not God but mammon. Inside the Bible he'd put all these obscene photos. I thought 42nd Street was bad. This guy has a real collection. Can you imagine tits and crotches facing a page of Scripture? It makes my unholy blood boil. Plus it's a little disgusting in and of itself. Do you think I can now blackmail him into getting another room? Before last weekend when he was away, I hadn't really fully understood or realized how marvelous it was not to have him around.

"Let me hear from you soon about these happenings. Betty's not really so bad, but I don't seem to be able to verbalize how I feel about her. Or about Sally. Or what difference there is between them. Fondly, Henry."

So much for Henry's not being very good with girls.

4

THIS IS ALL very difficult for me to comprehend.

I cannot quite picture Henry, in his rumpled Army surplus body, as the Casanova of Ohio. But on the other hand, I can imagine, neither can he. Yet he certainly handled himself well. I have to admit that it seems to have worked out O.K. It strikes me as being a bit far-fetched that any girl would really do that to me. (*For me?*)

I wonder if he'll be able to do his work. Guess he will. Henry suffers only from a creative diarrhea of the mind. I, on the other hand, am totally constipated when it comes to writing, or, as they say, "expressing" myself. Even the blankness of a white piece of typing paper is enough to frighten me. I have been known to sit for hours just staring into space, a word or two (like "The Pharaohs built . . ." or "The bimodal . . ." or even "Henry the Eighth held the . . .") typed out. I even went so far, once in high school, as to have left the paper in the typewriter for a whole week. It remained rigidly curled, to my embarrassment, even to the day the papers were handed back. Another thing about the differences between Henry and me, Henry could wait until the last minute to do a paper. Not me. I would get the assignment and then start to collect data as soon as the library doors opened the next day. I would be finished, in my own sluggish fashion, at least two days ahead of time. Henry believed that the more research you did, the more confused you got. So he would go home, get out the encyclopedia, and then write five pages. Never more, never less. He would hand it in on time, but his eyes *always* had circles under them. And we *always* got the same mark. While I *always* made points for accuracy, I lost on expression or grammar or something. With Henry it was the opposite — credit for an original idea, praise for his ability to make his points clearly, but *always* some criticism about his source material, attention to detail, and the like. I used to kid him that he was busiest while he was asleep. Me. I'm a squirrel. Well, he may be right. I spend a great deal of time getting ready to study. Actually it's a matter of focusing my attention. Since I never have worried about my marks — they've always been good

— I don't want to worry about them now. But I don't think I can avoid it.

"Dear Henry," I begin, "Jesus Christ! *The Knack* and all that. Sounds like that scene in *Blow-Up*. You ask me for advice? I'm sitting here in my nice, damp, little plastic tower like any other freshman in the world, sniffing my armpits and horny as hell. Also lonely. Can't communicate with anyone. My roommate Ted — nice guy, very New England — has gone off to join the SDS or something. The posters! Jesus, every foot of his side of the room (meaning the side I have to look at) is covered with all sorts of up-the-establishment-type monstrosities. Every time he sees an article on the Revolution, he tears it out of my *Times*. My very own *TIMES!!!* For which I had to pay something like $30 to have delivered here. Do you know what else he's done? (You'll like this. In the john, which we share with some other guys, he's pasted a photo of the President. And on the seat he painted *Kiss-ing her _ _ _*. Complete with illustrations. Oh yes, he's let his hair grow a foot and if he doesn't wear his glasses he looks like one hell of a freaked-out girl. I'm really worried. Like he's never seen any of this stuff before. He comes from a small town and this is his first time out, you know? So all of this radical nonsense is very potent for him. Like the first time we tried to smoke a cigarette, remember? Three weeks ago he hadn't heard of Che Guevera. Now he thinks he *is* Che Guevera. It's as though he's been in a cave all his life, and now

57

that he's come out to take a look at the world, he doesn't know what to make of it. Then when he looks around he sees that not only is it a lousy world, but somebody closed off the cave door. That metaphor stinks, I know, but before he works this thing out for himself, I'm afraid he'll be high on destruction and unable to get down. His perspective seems to be off, even about things like his parents. (He thinks they're bourgeois . . .) Well, you know the scene. I'm not so sure I understand what's going on. Do you? Advice, please, Abby.

"Upon rereading this letter, I think it stinks. Upon rereading your letter, I think you made up the whole thing. By the way, are you going to blackmail your roommate? What fun! . . . Please say hello to Sally for me. She sounds more your type than Betty. But who knows? Beware the bitch, or as they say in Latin, Cave canem. Enclosed is a list of speakers coming to the Boston area this year. I've circled a few you might like. I'm hoping that maybe you could come out here. Got to mail this with the last pickup. Better go. Keep cool."

I fold up the letter and slip it into an airmail envelope. It's not a very good letter, I admit, but at least it's something. It's rotten when people don't write back. Luckily, that's not one of Henry's weaknesses. It is mine.

So I dash over to the post office and then go to dinner. The place is kind of empty because it's still early. I don't see anyone I know except for Ted who's way off in a corner with about five other guys. An interesting unit — like a cell. It occurs to me that that might be just what the group might be about. So I am about to sit down alone when I see my chemistry professor. Since chemistry, to put it mildly, is not my best subject, at first I hesitate. After all, he is a professor. What would I talk about? What would he think — that I'm sitting with him just because he's my professor and I want to chalk up some extra points? What's more, would he even recognize me?

As I am deliberating he looks up and sees me. He waves at me to come sit down.

Dr. Yankaskas is a nice guy. He's not too old, sort of thin, and pale with thin reddish hair and horn-rimmed glasses. Very much what any professor ought to look like. Tweedy, you might say. When he lectures, his accent — Russian, I would guess — is very slight unless someone asks him a question and he gets nervous and it gets thick.

As I come over to where he is sitting, he starts clearing away his books and hat and things that are on the table. "You're Schoen, aren't you?" I nod. "Second row. Terrible way to remember students, isn't it?"

"No. How's the food tonight?" I am busy getting myself set to eat. This entails putting the coat on a chair, the books under the table, the plates off the tray and onto the table, the tray off to one side.

"Dinner? Oh, tolerable. Not Durgin Park, certainly, but tolerable."

"Do you eat at school often?" I ask, not really caring.

"No, just when I'm working on something."

"This must seem pretty rotten to you. I mean, we get used to it after a while, but I guess you have a wife at home, huh?"

"Well, I suppose you could say that. She's a chemist, too. But she does cook. We both cook, actually."

"Do you eat Russian food?" I ask, knowing instantly I had made a faux pas.

"Russian? No. I am Lithuanian, and she is Latvian. We eat a mélange of foods. French, Italian, Slavic . . . you name it."

"Did you meet here in this country?"

"No. We met at the Sorbonne. Then the war came and I didn't see her for a while and then she turned up in Rome when I was there. We got married in England. A very extended courtship, you might say."

"Is this supposed to be roast beef?" I ask, a little surprised how closely the flavor simulated shoe leather.

"Yes," he says, his eyes narrowing slightly as if in disapproval.

I decide not to talk about how terrible it tastes because I have made this mistake before with relatives who were refugees from various political turmoils. No matter how much time passes, they can never let you forget that at one time they would have sold their souls for a loaf of bread. Quickly I ask, "Are you doing research at the library?"

"Yes. I'm working on a short paper for a small environmental journal."

60

(A journal for small environments? I think, paren-thetically.)

"It's a simple paper, but I make a rule of never dis-cussing my work until it's finished. It keeps the edge on my interest. Remember that if you're ever working on a long term paper. Then, if I feel that the basic work is done, I give it to my wife to read. But she's the only one. After it's finished, I give it to a friend who polishes the English and then I mail it off. Very simple. Unfortunately, I'm not a very good writer. I don't think many scientists are, in this country. What's equally unfortunate is that we are almost forced to produce papers and lectures in order to sur-vive. So what happens is that the only people to profit from all this scientific business are the paper companies. Certainly the publishers never make any profit. My wife is an invaluable aid. She's a good critic and she has many good ideas."

My mind is somewhere hovering in midair. Mar-cuse suddenly comes to my mind. Not that I've read more than ten pages of his work. "Have you read Marcuse?"

He looks as though he is about to say no, when a man appears at our side. He is tall and slender, with dark thinning hair, mustache, and glasses. I've seen him around — probably one of the professors. He is carrying a cup of tea.

"John . . ."

"Hello, hello."

"Hi. I just came over to congratulate you on your grant."

"Thank you."

"Or should I say, *latest* grant?" he asks, smiling. He pulls up a chair and sits. "Very good work. Very good. I read a summary and it's . . . Oh, hello," he says, noticing me.

I nod, saying nothing.

Turning back to Dr. Y., he says, "I'd like to discuss something with you. Are you free on Tuesday afternoon, say about three o'clock?"

"Yes. Perfect. What about?"

"Oh, something of interest to both of us." He pauses to change the subject. His brown eyes change from very serious to self-mocking. "You'll never guess what happened last weekend."

Dr. Y. smiled.

"I drove out to the Cape in the Jeep with the kids and Ann. We went to the wildlife preserve because I wanted to check some data on water levels and fowl and such for a paper I'm to read soon. Been working on it for a while — you know, for that conference. Anyway" — he smacks his lips in self-disgust — "we drove around for a while on trails and narrow dirt roads and then we got deep into a part of the preserve where you're not supposed to be."

"No."

"Yes, and then we saw a lot of signs saying *No Entry* and things like that so we went on until we found a path that seemed to go out onto the shore where I wanted to go. For samples and things."

"Yes."

"As we drove, it became apparent that we were getting deeper and deeper in the mud. But I was too smart to turn around. No. I kept on telling Ann that it would get better because there was more sand out toward the water and such."

"Uh-huh."

"And then when I really thought it was going to be bad, I decided to find a way of turning around. That may have been my mistake, because I think if I hadn't stopped, our momentum would have kept us going."

"But you stopped."

"Right."

"And you and your kids and your wife were all stuck." Dr. Y. is grinning sarcastically.

"Right."

"In your Jeep station wagon, four-wheel-drive deluxe special camping car."

"That's not all" — he was smiling too — "We were trying to rock ourselves out and then came some guy — probably just as overconfident as me — in a heavier truck, and he was trying to pull us out . . ."

"But he got stuck too!" Dr. Y. was laughing and laughing.

" Yes, but that's still not all. Calm yourself, John!"

"I'm trying to . . ."

"So, there we were, my kids whining, my wife on the verge of tears, nothing in sight, no telephone lines, nothing. So I took one of the boys with me and we tromped up the road where we could see an old house. It wasn't too far away, so we walked along the shore and got there and rang the bell. The house must have been there before the preserve was sealed off. This tired dirty-looking woman answered the bell. She and her son — who looked slightly retarded — must live there alone."

"Sounds like something out of Tennessee Williams," Dr. Y. puts in.

"Yes. And she let us use the phone. Then we walked back to the Jeep. We killed about an hour talking before the tow truck found us."

"You got towed out?"

"Yes. And it cost a small fortune, believe me."

"Ha ha ha ha." Tears are running down Dr. Y.'s cheeks.

"And then — wait, John, you haven't heard the best part! Then, as soon as we had paid off this tow truck, a guard or whatever you call him came slinking up and sheepishly walked over to us and rather apologetically gave us a summons for destroying public property!"

The two of them are now roaring. Dr. Y. barely has the breath to ask, "And what's the judge going to say when you tell him that you're an environmental scientist?"

"I don't know! I don't know! He'll probably throw the book at me!"

"Terrific. Terrific. I can't wait to tell everyone about this at the conference!"

"Oh, John, you wouldn't. That's just a story between friends. My ego is shattered."

"I can tell. What about Ann? Was she mad?"

"A little. To console everybody we went out for dinner. Just to add to the expense."

"Ah, you poor thing."

"Right." After a pause, he adds, "Well, got to go. I have to go back to the office to grade some papers, then to the library."

"See you," Dr. Y. says, draining his tea and wiping his lips with a paper napkin. The other man leaves quickly, without further conversation. As if to fill in, Dr. Y. says to me, "Speaking of work, I'd best get back to mine . . . Ready?"

I say I am, and we collect ourselves and our belongings from sundry chairs. On the way over we talk, and he tells me that I should come over to his house sometime for a beer. I tell him that I will. Sometime. We stop in front of the library door. In a soft voice he says, "I am afraid, David. These radicals. What do they understand of a man's devotion to his work? They want to destroy certain evils in society. Reformers with bombs. Who ever heard of anything more absurd?"

"I believe," I say, afraid that he might misinterpret my own political leanings, "that they feel that the scientific community has sold out, wholesale, to the establishment. The radicals want to punish scientists for this, without much attention to individuals."

"Punish? Punish? What about slumlords and, and . . ."

"True, but they're not supposed to be very bright."

"How Jesuitical! To those who have been given

65

much, much will be expected." He snorts. He opens the heavy door. "We'd better get going. Please do drop by the house sometime. We live in the only blue house on Elizabeth Street. It's a short street over toward Harvard Square."

We part at the elevator. "I enjoyed tonight's conversation," he says, and we nod good-bye to each other as he steps in.

I think about all the stuff Ted has been giving me, about dialogue being the lost essence of education. About how too much of what goes on is involved with mere facts. Even sex, he claims, isn't just fluids being passed from one body to another. That's just what you tell yourself, he says, when you can't afford to care. But it is a dialogue, too. At least that's what he says. But I guess all New Englanders are puritans.

I settle myself in one of the hard wooden chairs in the reading room. What do I know, I ask myself, flipping open my notebook. Sex, revolution, science. Supposedly the three basic commodities of my life here. And only four years to figure them out. Are they that basic? Henry would probably say no. He'd probably interject that life is art, not science. Oh Janis Joplin. Oh Jimi Hendrix. *Ora Pro Nobis.*

5

IT IS RAINING OUT. It has been raining for three days and my bones ache with it. I creak out of bed and dress. I cannot remember what has awakened me. Perhaps the flushing of a john. Nothing romantic like a skylark. There are no such animals. Keats. Shelley. All heads. All completely stoned.

There is nothing about the day that is romantic. It is a perfectly awful Boston/Cambridge day. Somehow I survive the walk over to the dining hall — it's only a few hundred feet, actually. I check the mail before I go up to eat. I bend low, squinting into the dark little square hole and think I see nothing. Then

I see a slim line of a silhouette. I pull it out. It is a postcard. A picture of some painting. There is no signature, but the postmark is Cleveland, Ohio. All it says is: "*The heart's eye grieves/Discovering you, dark tramplers, tyrant years.* G. M. Hopkins."

The fine print on the back says that it is a portrait of a young man, anonymous Dutch, 1600s, collection, Cleveland Museum of Art. I turn over the card and study the picture. I study the face for a long time before I stick it into my notebook. The face is Ted's.

I guess I'll never be able to figure out how Henry does these things.

6

It is a gray Sunday and I am with Ted walking through the Boston Common. There is to be a speaker there, according to the student paper, that Ted wants to hear. We walk briskly, glancing at the organ grinder and his monkey, the strolling Bostonians out for their Sunday constitutionals, and assorted freaks. I am surprised at Ted for asking me to come along. I would have expected that he might have just disappeared for the day, and come back to the room without saying anything about what he had done. It's terrible. I really like Ted. I could be his friend, if only he would trust me. Stupid me, I suppose. I could be as close to him as I am to Henry, but Ted keeps pushing me away. Pushing, pushing, quietly and firmly. Henry has never been able to keep too much to himself. Sometimes it's as though he were forced by his own nature to keep revealing himself. Like his letters. But Ted is his polar opposite. Sad. But at the same time, I had resolved — before I came to college, the night before, in fact, lying in bed thinking of what it would be like and all and not being able to sleep — to accept people the way they are, and not try to impose any kind of condition on my friendships. High school was so full of that. Pettiness, as my folks would say. Some of my friends used to pick on Henry behind his back. They couldn't accept his idiosyncrasies with his good qualities, and maybe even his good qualities they were not mature enough to appreciate.

And so Ted and I are moving together along the same sidewalk at the same point in time and yet we're so far apart.

We are going to hear this speaker, and I have already started to brace myself against him. He is a Black Panther officer, wanted by the FBI. He had announced publicly that he would give himself up at the rally today, and has already begun to speak when we arrive. There is a large crowd of people around the band shell. We sit on the slope. The speaker's ideas are interesting and his style flawless. I find myself caught up in the spirit of his polemics, even though I know, intellectually, that he's not really saying anything new. The audience is filled with young Panthers, students, and a handful of older blacks. There are several other white faces, half of which Ted asserts are FBI men. There are also about 100 uniformed cops on the rims of the Common. From our elevated position we can see the street beyond us filled with police cars parked like animals about to spring. Since this rally has propaganda value for both police and Panthers, there is some kind of arrangement by which the cops are going to let him speak for a few minutes before arresting him.

Without any warning, or, it seems to us, any provocation, suddenly the Panthers are fighting with the cops, sirens blare, and we are surrounded by patrol cars. Ted runs over to join some other students. I am trying to see what is going on and to make sure that nobody has decided to start shooting. The police herd a group of people toward me, so I start to move myself down the hill. I don't want to get arrested, so I try to look as though I am cooperating. A policeman stops me. He looks angry enough to kick the shit out of me. "Where're you going, kid?" he snarls.

I have read The Naked Ape and I am trying to look submissive. I bow my head a little and clasp my hands together over my racing heart. "Back to campus, sir."

Just as I thought, he likes this. He smiles stiffly. "O.K., kid, get out of here as fast as you can or I'll kick the shit out of you."

Just as I suspected.

I race down the slope and make for the MTA station on the corner. I stop to look for Ted, but it's impossible. The area begins to look like a battle zone.

Every siren in Massachusetts is converging on the Common. I get on the subway. I decide to go over to Harvard Square. Maybe Ted will be there. Besides, I want to buy a *Times*. Ted gave mine away this morning to one of his friends.

The *Times* I buy provides a nice seat. I go up to Harvard's administration complex at Holyoke. I am sitting reading the book review section, every now and then looking to see if Ted has arrived or if anyone I know has shown up. Finally I spot a guy who lives across the hall from us. I go over to him. "Hey, Gerry."

"Yeah?"

"You at the rally?" I ask. "At the Common?"

"Yeah. Didn't see you. Did you hear about Ted?"

"No. Got separated."

"Yeah. Figured. Ted got busted."

"I could have guessed," I say nervously.

"Uh-uh. I mean literally. Pigs busted his head open. Shoved him into some ambulance. Looked bad." Gerry shook his head. "Man, they were rough bastards today. Didn't expect this."

"What hospital did they take him to?"

"Mass. General."

I start to go. "I'm going over there. Want to come?"

"Why? What can we do for him?"

"Nothing, I suppose," I murmur. "But I still feel I should go. Suppose his parents call?"

"Mmm. Yes." Gerry nods his head slowly.

"Hey, there's going to be a rally at five to protest

police brutality." Some jock-looking guy is talking over my shoulder, yelling into my ear like it's a birthday party he's talking about.

"Where?" Gerry asks.

"Here. Stick around, man." The jock zips off.

Gerry looks at me. "Think I'll stay. See you later when you get back."

"Yeah," I say, walking over to the trolley stop.

7

I SIT IN THE BLEAK WAITING ROOM of the hospital. I sit until I think I can no longer take it. I tell every nurse that walks in that I want to see Ted. Finally one of them brings me over to a corridor, points, and says, "See that cop. He's in charge of the arrested patients. Talk to him."

I go over to him. He gives me a long look and waits for me to speak. I am nervous and he knows it. "I heard that my roommate was hurt and I came to see if there was anything I could do for him or his parents."

It was as though I hadn't said anything. "Are you a student, my lad?"

74

"Yes sir."

"Harvard?" He asks, his eyes curling.

"No, M.I.T., sir."

"Oh, a scientist."

"Yessir. Is my roommate . . ."

"My son is your age." He paused for a long breath, then he added, "He's in Vietnam." His eyes stabbed into mine.

He takes me over to a door with a glass window. He points. "Is that your friend?"

I look in. Ted is just lying there, eyes shut. There is blood caked on his hair, his neck, his jacket, the sheets. There are even drops of blood on the floor. I feel weak, like I'm going to faint. So I turn away and lean against the cool green wall. "Can't they stitch him up?"

"They could. But there are many other people in this room who need help, too. Folks who don't go around throwing rocks at policemen."

So that was it. I murmur something under my breath.

Finally a nurse comes to the door. "This kid over here, Sergeant. He's unconscious. No I.D. What do we do with him?"

"You mean this guy over here?" He points to Ted. She nods. "His roommate is here. You want him to identify him?"

She nods again. The cop looks at me, hard. "Now, your identification will only be final when his parents come down, but you'll help us a great deal if you tell us all you know about him."

"I'm only his roommate. We're freshmen. We didn't pick each other. Don't think that I . . ."

"Yeah, we know, kid." He propels me through the door. A nurse is standing next to Ted with a form ready.

"Can't you stitch him up?" I look down on the blood and his twisted expression.

"He'll be all right," she says impatiently. Her pencil is poised. "Name?"

"His or mine?" I ask.

"His, then yours."

"He's Ted Holmes. I'm David Schoen. We're both freshmen at M.I.T." She gets all that down. I continue, "His parents live in Seabury, Maine. It's a small town and you probably can find them right away." I had thought of giving the wrong information but that wouldn't help anyone in the end and would probably get me into a lot of trouble. The nurse leaves to look up his parents' phone number. I turn to the cop. "Do I have to speak with his parents?"

"Don't you think it would be better than getting it from a total stranger?"

"Do I have to tell them about Ted's being arrested?"

"It might be a lot simpler if they get it all over with now."

His reply is so calm that it knocks me over practically. He's done this before. Hundreds of times. It must keep on happening, too. "Hello, madam, this is a policeman and your son has been shot."

"Hello, sir, this is a policeman and your daughter is here in the withdrawal tank screaming."

The room is filled with people in white. The light is harsh. I stand near Ted. His glasses are gone; his hair is thick with blood. I hear him moan. "Ted," I say.

The nurse trots back, her white nylons singing as she walks. Her uniform rustles clean. She has the number written down on a piece of paper. She dials from a nearby phone and then hands the phone over to me. "Let me talk before the sergeant," she says.

I hear the phone ringing. I am numb. I haven't even started to rehearse what to say. The rings are long and finally a man answers, "Hello?"

"Hello. Mr. Holmes?"

"Yes?"

"This is David Schoen, Ted's roommate."

"Yes, David?"

"Mr. Holmes, I'm terribly sorry to have to call you . . ."

"What's wrong?"

"Well, sir, Ted was injured this afternoon in a demonstration. Not too seriously, sir, but they are stitching him up at Massachusetts General Hospital. I'm with him."

"Oh dear. Dear." His voice suddenly calls out to his wife. "Momma, come here!" He clears his throat. "Excuse me, David. He's all right, though, you say?"

"Yes, sir, except that, unfortunately, he's been arrested, too. I'm sorry."

"Arrested?" I hear Ted's mother gasp in the background. "No, no. That's not possible. He didn't do anything bad, not Ted. Did you see what happened?"

"No, sir," I decided to lie for the benefit of the fuzz at my elbow. "I wasn't there. But there's a nurse who must speak with you and then a policeman will tell you about his charges. I'd better go now."

"Yes. Thank you, David. You stay by our boy. We'll work this thing out somehow."

"Good-bye, sir."

The nurse takes over now. Covering the mouthpiece of the telephone, she whispers, "Good work." She is almost smiling. She has to get her forms filled out. All that information about insurance, parental permission. I go over closer to Ted. I put my hand on his arm. His eyes open slightly. They seem to focus. I tell him where he is, that he's been arrested, that his parents are on the phone. I ask if he can talk to them. His eyes are blank. Completely blank. But he keeps staring at me. I tell him things will be all right. Not to worry.

An intern comes over and shoves me aside. He starts cleaning up. The wound is under Ted's hair, so the intern starts to clip away a patch. The sergeant comes back from the phone. "Why don't you cut it all off?" He says loudly. Ted shuts his eyes. The sergeant turns to me. "It's a shame. Those poor parents. They're very nice people. They don't deserve to suffer this."

I guess he's right. I don't say anything. I am watching the intern thread a needle. "I'd better be going." I look at Ted. I feel utterly helpless. I go outside the emergency room with the sergeant. Back to the green sterile corridor. "Will the school be notified?"

"Yes, certainly."

"May I come to see him tomorrow?"

"You could try, but I'm sure he'll be locked up in the Prison Ward until he's better or until his parents come and bail him out. He's lucky. The beds are softer here than they are in jail." He chuckles to himself.

I go back to school. I walk a lot of the way along the river. The Charles is like ink. Ted will probably be suspended from school. His medical expenses, his legal fees, his tuition, all down the drain. And his time, eroding, fleeing, wasting itself in jail or whatever. The uncertainty of it all. What if he should go to jail? Then what? What would I do if it were me they arrested? I can't go to jail, I have too many plans. And time off in jail is not one of them. I have to do four years of undergraduate work and then seven more years in school between my Master's and my Ph.D. Then I would need a few years to get a start. When would real life start? I wouldn't ever be finished. Jail! Man, I couldn't ever afford to get arrested. Not without some reason, some purpose. But on the other hand, I'm never going to take any risks. Society is blackmailing me, making success the only important thing in life. Is this life? No direction, no feeling, just ambition?

I get onto the bus that crosses over to Cambridge. I sit down sadly and lean my head against the window. The bus is dirty and old and it makes me feel uncomfortable, the way I feel around my senile grandmother. Repulsed and guilty for feeling repulsion — all mixed up.

Time makes suckers out of all of us.

8

Ted's not being in the room somehow does make a difference. It shouldn't, but it does. The atmosphere is less tense. I get a lot of work done and things are going so well I decide to get off campus for a while. After much hesitation, I start out for Dr. Yankaskas' house. I walk. It's not too far. I rationalize why I'm not calling first: because I don't want them to not go out or do something because I'm coming, or go and get anything ready like beer or Cokes. (It's something that comes from having my mother always saying she never knows which she prefers: having an excuse for general messiness or having only half an hour's notice to clean up two days' worth of junk.) But actually I want to see how professors live. I want to see if they have pipe collections and Marilyn Monroe wives and 4000 books. I want to see if there are books in the refrigerator and shaving cream in the liquor cabinet. Or if there's a TV set or if the opera will be playing on the stereo.

I arrive. I ring the bell and a small boy answers the door. I don't really know much about kids. This one looks like he might be ten or so. I ask, "Is Dr. Yankaskas at home?"

"Yeah. Come in. I'll call him." He runs inside and up the stairs two at a time. "Hey Dad. Dad! A student's here to see you!"

I come inside and close the door behind me. My feet are wet and so I don't step off the mat by the door. Hearing the professor's steps coming downstairs, I look up. Out of the corner of my eye, I see that a door opens off the dining room and a woman in an apron is also converging upon me. They arrive at the same time, saying hello, how are you, and all that. The professor introduces me to his wife, who in her apron looks much more like a wife than a chemist. Before we get much done as far as helping me out of my coat and putting me someplace like on the sofa in the living room, there is a crash in the kitchen. Mrs. Y. makes a beeline for the kitchen and we all follow. We find a small blond girl wiping up a puddle on the floor with paper towels and scolding a sedate cat who shows signs of wanting to share in the cleaning-up process. "Bad kitty," she was saying as we entered.

"What did kitty do?" Dr. Y. asks.

"She wanted to taste my brownies but she wouldn't wait until I finished *baking* them." She looked embarrassed.

"Don't pick up those small pieces of the bowl. I'll do it," her father said. Everyone was smiling. "This is David, one of my students. This is my daughter, Mara." He starts to clean up the broken pieces.

Mara gets up and shakes my hand. We stand in the kitchen and talk, all of us, as dinner is being made, each of us making something. I work on the salad. It never occurs to me that I am going to stay for dinner. It doesn't occur to me, nor to them, to mention it. We talk and joke through dinner, clear the table, and I take my leave, thanking them. I am halfway home when I realize that I've made such a fool out of myself. But, I think to myself, everything was so much fun, so much like a real family, that it was worth it. I decide to write them a note as soon as I get back to the dorm.

9

TED COMES BACK to school. His status here is pending a hearing, as far as the school goes. He is released from the clutches of the law on an absurdly large bond. The Civil Liberties Union is taking on the case against the ten kids who were involved. The whole thing has become a big deal. I know it sounds rotten, but Ted's return to school has messed up my life and I wish he hadn't been allowed back. I have to put up with a *cause célèbre* for a roommate. At first it is fairly interesting — lots of phone calls from reporters and magazine writers, but now it is getting to be, as Henry would say, a bore. Not only do all the radicals of the Boston metropolis flock to our room, but every time a C.L.U. lawyer-type comes by to talk to Ted, I have to leave the room. Ted isn't even studying and has begun to play a role, sort of a turned-on Bogart. It would have been better for everyone if he had been suspended.

They are all pleading not guilty. They are claiming that they were all standing peaceably about when policemen started to beat them up, and that the so-called "assault" was merely self-defense. Exhibit A, broken glasses; exhibit B, stitches. It might even be true, and it probably wouldn't be the first time it's happened. But all the same, everybody's decided to hate everybody else. Even Ted's parents pulled a switch. They've more or less rejected him. They came down to bail him out and stand by him, so to speak, but all the thanks they got was a few shrugs of the shoulders from him. Besides, they couldn't quite hassle the police-brutality charge. To them, policemen are still the Men in Blue who guard their lives and property from harm. Especially property. They went back to Maine, to its snow and icicles and maple syrup and frozen ponds, and left behind our polluted revolution.

Meanwhile, things between Ted and me grow worse. He knows that there's a limit to what I can take, and so he keeps pushing. Finally, late at night, I come back from the small study room where I have been going to escape from this nonsense. As I open the door, I get the feeling that I am definitely interrupting something. The room is filled with acrid smoke and there are about six guys there huddled in the middle of the floor. Heads turn around and glare at me. Ted stands up.

"Well, well, David. Turning in early?" He is all sarcasm. I am a bit frightened. "Yeah," I say. "This is my room, isn't it? I mean, I haven't made a mistake or anything?"

"No. Come in. Come in, my boy." He extends his hand and gives a mock bow.

The voices from the floor object, "Hey, Ted . . . No, man. No. Keep him out."

"No, no," Ted says quietly. "It's my fault for not letting old Dave here know what's going on. He is my roommate, after all, and he probably thinks I'm rude not to include him. So we will. David, come here. I want you to see what we're doing."

I come closer. On the floor are maps of the city. There are several lines and circles drawn on them. I pull back, not wanting to look, but looking anyway. Knowing but not wanting to know what they meant. My breath grows short, my voice quakes. "Please, Ted, I'm going. Please don't show me anything, don't tell me anything. I don't want to know." I turn to run, but Ted's voice stops me.

"David, you probably know already what we're doing, so there's no point in trying to pretend that you're innocent." He says this coolly.

"Innocent. Of what?" My hands and face are damp with hot perspiration.

"You know everything we're doing because there's been some messing around with my letters and notes. You did it."

"I certainly did not. I don't meddle in other people's affairs. What good would it do me?"

"Maybe it won't do you any good, but somebody would be very interested in what we're doing and able to pay a good price to find it out."

"Don't be ridiculous!" I shout. "You think anybody else would take you punks seriously? You're out of your mind!"

"Who the hell do you think you are, Schoen?" There was a pause in his venom. The room was vibrating with hate. "You're such a nice little Jewish boy, you wouldn't understand, would you? Well, look at this." He thrusts the maps under my nose. "You know what these are. You know what our plans are. You know all about our bombs."

"No. I don't know, and I don't want to know. Leave me alone!"

"You're lying. You've been spying all this time. But I'll tell you this once. If anything happens, any mysterious tip-offs, we'll know who did it, and one of us will get you." He was raving.

"Don't try it, Ted. Don't even bother. Your infantile plots don't interest me. They're all in your mind. You don't have the guts to try anything. Revolution, my ass. Grow up." I start down the hall to find somebody on whose floor I can sleep tonight and I hear Ted scream after me . . .

"You ingratiating sniveling puny little kike!"

It takes all my self-control to keep walking. Like a kick in the groin, his words make me want to puke.

10

I SPEND THE REST of the week dodging Ted, sleeping on couches, floors, sleeping bags. Friday I get so depressed I decide to go to some beer party in one of the dorms. The girls at these things are always terrible. At least the ones I wind up talking with are. I just can't seem to learn how to stop talking to ugly girls and cut out when a good-looking one comes along. It kills me to be rude. I have a lot of ugly cousins, and so I feel sorry for all ugly girls. I used to think once that pretty girls were stupid and ugly girls were smart. That was before I started going to these beer parties and started talking with ugly girls all night.

I think of Henry and all those women, apparently all beautiful, all throwing themselves at him. And Henry's such a weird-looking guy. And then I think of me and all these ugly girls. I get even more depressed.

I go anyway. One of these ugly girls starts talking about cannibalism and the Holy Eucharist and how cannibalism in some tribal cultures is considered a form of reverent ancestor worship. Well, I saw *Satyricon*, too, and when her warm, damp hand touches me on the arm and she starts talking about how that's why lovers bite each other, I start to feel the beer turn into a small churning ocean in my stomach. She sees my face turning green, I am sure, so I dash for the john without even attempting to excuse myself. Afterwards I feel weak, but a lot better. I also taste that terrible stuff in my mouth and decide that I'd better find something to eat to cover it up.

I go down the street, looking for something cold and sweet, like ice cream. Two girls walk by. They are eating strawberry ice-cream cones. I stop them. I keep my mouth covered with my hand and ask them where they got the cones. Around the corner at Brigham's, they say. One of them asks why I'm covering my mouth. Because, I say, I just threw up about a pitcher of beer. They laugh. They are both pretty.

"Here, have a bite," says one of them. "That's a terrible mouth to have to live with even for a few minutes."

"Thanks," I say, but before I can do anything, the other one interrupts.

"Hey, you can have *all* of mine. I'm really not supposed to be eating this stuff."

"Why not?" I ask, taking the cone.

"Because I'm fat," she says, giggling.

"Oh, you are not," the other girl says.

"I don't care. You've given me some ice cream, that's all that counts. And if it doesn't matter to me, well, then what difference can a few calories make?" My depression vanishes with the fine pink taste of the ice cream.

"Hey, you're a nice guy! This is Sheila," she adds smoothly, "and I'm Hannah."

"My name is David," I say, conscious of leaving off my last name. "Where are you going?"

"Just around. Want to come?" Hannah asks.

We walk around. They ask me where I'm from and I tell them, they ask me where I'm going to school and I tell them. They ask me about some superficial things. I don't ask them much. The cone is about finished and we seem to be running out of things to say. Then we find ourselves at one of the magazine stores near Harvard Square. We each buy something, after about twenty minutes of leafing through things and poking around. I buy *Crawdaddy*, which I used to subscribe to but which I haven't seen in several months. They buy *Art News* and two other small literary journals. I'm not at all into poetry.

Sheila flips one open. It has THE IOWA STATE LIQUOR STORE printed across the cover. I gather that that's the name of it, ludicrous as it seems. "Look, Hannah, Ike's poem is in this one!"

Hannah peeks over Sheila's shoulder. "Hey, let's see. Oh, he didn't say anything about it." She pauses to read a few lines to herself. "Hey, this is the one he wrote after that thing with Louise. Wow." She looks up. "Hey, what about some coffee? We're almost home."

"Or we could go to the coffee shop and get something . . ." Sheila says.

"Oh, but it's not the same, and David should see your place."

We walk along the dark streets. We talk a bit about life in Cambridge. We halt before a dark, low building while Sheila hunts through her jeans pockets for the key. We go down a few steps and then she opens the door to her basement studio. Studio in more than one sense: there are paint tubes and brushes in turpentine and canvas rolls all over.

We go in. Sheila disappears behind a curtain and soon the smell of coffee floats through the air. Meanwhile, Hannah and I settle ourselves among the pillows and mattresses on the floor. The apartment is old and spacious. It has high ceilings and a fireplace. There is no furniture except for pillows and low Chinese tables. The lighting comes from cylindrical tubes twisting light up and over and around the room. I look around. Hannah gets up and pushes aside some paintings. A stereo appears. Then she puts on a record and from the shadows comes the music of, well, I suppose it could only be Italian Renaissance church music. The tone is pure. I guess that the amplifiers are A/R. Sheila comes back, her arms loaded with a trayful of coffee things. We sit cross-legged and watch silently as Sheila pours. There are pastry-shop cookies, little napkins, and sterling teaspoons. The finesse with which it is doled out makes me smile.

Pointing to where I guess the amplifiers are hanging, I say to Sheila, "Somebody loves you."

"Oh, yes. Well, they're not exactly mine. A friend of mine lives here some of the time and they're his."

"I see." I'm not exactly sure what I'm supposed to have said.

"It's perfectly sordid, I suppose. He really comes around to visit only when he wants to see if there are any paint spots on his cabinet over there." Sheila smiles.

"That's not true, and you know it. He's madly in love with you," Hannah protests.

"Is that what he tells you? Come on . . ."

"You don't take Jason very seriously . . ."

"Neither does Jason. He's still tinkering around with hi-fis and old cars. The only thing that saves him is that he doesn't wear white socks."

"Well, he never wears shoes . . ."

"Oh, he certainly does. I just don't let him around here, but most of the time he runs around in a suit and a tie and shoes and socks. I'm pretty sure he doesn't wear underwear, though. He's leading a double life." She pauses. "How inconsiderate of us. David doesn't know what we're talking about and probably wouldn't care if he did."

"That's not true. In any case it's refreshing to listen to people talk, even when it's about nothing in particular." I then proceed to tell them all about Ted. The coffee is finished and we continue to talk. Hannah falls asleep. Sheila and I continue. Somewhere along the line I figure out how to tell Sheila from Hannah. Sheila is slightly older, has a more pointed chin, and must be ten pounds thinner than Hannah. But they both have long reddish-brown hair, pale skin, the same fierce blue eyes, and are wearing pretty much the same things: jeans and embroidered Mexican shirts. There are only slight other differences: for instance, Sheila's nose is shorter than Hannah's.

Sheila discusses her work, how Hannah hates Radcliffe, why I would ever want to be a psychoanalyst. Sheila is still willing to continue, but I announce that I'd better go.

"Where?" Sheila asks pointedly. "Why not stay here? There are plenty of mattresses."

"I have work to do," I say, wondering if Sheila was really a Betty come flashing in from Ohio to play a joke on me.

"Oh, come on. You can go back after breakfast." I smile, but hesitate for a minute. "Come on," she repeats. "Besides, Hannah likes you." She smiles benevolently at the slumped figure of her sister. I say O.K., and we find some pillows and a blanket and I sack out on one of the mattresses.

11

And so I stay. I don't go back to the dorm until the next night and then, after thinking about it for a while, I leave again and bring my things over to Sheila's. It is awkward, I know. Suppose old what's-his-name comes over. Suppose people start looking for me at school. Still, I find it impossible to spend any more time with Ted, or near Ted, or near Ted's image.

Things work out well. Sheila doesn't expect Jason back until Saturday and she's willing to take me in until then. Hannah stays at her dorm, but she comes over to see me — and Sheila, I suppose. Sheila's not the kind to get hung up on details like dressing or undressing, and picking up socks. She's out most of the time, working at her studio over at the School of Fine Arts. I amble over to classes or hitch a ride with some guy in the building who's a grad student at M.I.T.

By the end of the week, I am feeling much better. I have two friends who are girls, instead of one all-time, Miss Everything girl friend. Things go free. There are no phone calls, first dates, and such. There are other people coming by when Sheila's there at night, so when I leave the library, I am propelled by my anticipation. No more of this Ted-depression. I know it has to end soon. The weekend comes and Sheila gets the word that Jason is coming by to pick her up and take her up to New Hampshire. Sheila rolls up a few stretchers in some canvas and hands me the key to the apartment. She goes off in the evening fog. I appreciate the weekend to myself. Hannah will be around. The pressure seems to cool off and I've gotten more work done than before. I am completely free of Ted and his gang. I do know which way the wind blows.

Things go pretty well. Thanksgiving is in sight. Maybe it's the weather, the damp Boston fall, or being in New England where it all started, or it could be Hannah and Sheila. I don't know, but Thanksgiving has never seemed like such a terrific idea before. Hannah and I go to the Common on the Saturday before Thanksgiving. We are thinking of just walking around, maybe buying a kite to fly. Or maybe we would go over to Back Bay and walk along the river.

Some friends live nearby. Sheila's friends, actually. Or one guy lives over on Charles Street. We might go to see him and look at the shops along the way. But when we get out of the subway, Hannah says, "Hey, David! Let's follow the feet!"

"What are you talking about, woman?" I say.

"The feet. The Liberty Trail or whatever they call it. I see them all the time and I've never figured out where they go. Please?"

And so we begin. We wind our way through history. Historic places, museums, houses, churches. One if by land, two if by sea, and all that. We go past banks and shoe shops and antique stores and down and around and in and out of monuments. We end up at Haymarket, then walk around into the Italian section.

We pass crowded windows and aromatic doorways. Sausages, cheeses all hanging in the dim light inside the stores. We browse and sneeze on the sawdust, and end up buying some olives and a chunk of cheese and then we find a bakery. We walk around some more until we find a spot to sit down.

"My nose is tired," Hannah says laughingly, as I tear into the bread. "Happy Thanksgiving!" She pops an olive in her mouth.

"Well, Turkey Day is a little ways off. Don't be overanxious. And what part of the great bird do you think you're eating, little girl?" She seems to enjoy being teased. "You know, my mother makes the most incredible stuffed turkey and things . . . I'm really looking forward to going home. The food here is so rotten — I mean at school. *This* stuff is terrific," I say.

"Here, have some provolone. Is that all you want to see your parents for — their food?" Hannah smiles, but underneath there is a certain grayness.

"No, no. I mean, I really like them. I miss them, actually. My mother is kind of crazy. Dad's O.K., but he tries to appear so straight. He's a lawyer. Guess he couldn't really be a real stiff. Not with Mom around." I bite into an olive. "I never asked you. Funny. Where do you live? I mean, where are your folks?"

Hannah looks away. "They were killed two years ago. Wherever Sheila is is home now."

It is so unexpected. And she is so sadly calm, as though she still misses them, yet is somehow satisfied. I can't say that I've never thought about my parents' deaths, but I can never imagine the years afterward, how it would be like to have no one there — the phone number that would have to be forgotten, the apartment key that would just lie in the back of some drawer of socks. "I'm sorry," I say. "That's terrible. I'm sorry I asked."

"No, don't be, David. They died together. It was quick, and they were together. From the letters that we've found, they must have been very much in love, even after eighteen years — in a kind of silly way. They were always funny. Yes, I think they were very much in love."

Too quickly, I ask, "Are you and Sheila going to stay here and spend Thanksgiving alone?"

97

"Well — I suppose I shouldn't tell you. Will you promise not to tell Sheila?" I nod, and cross my heart. "You see, Jason came by the other day and showed me this incredible ring that he had bought for Sheila. It was owned by some Medici. It's small and beautiful and she'll never say no to Jason anyway. So, since his parents are in New York, I guess what will happen is that we'll go down as soon as she says yes, which she will, and have Thanksgiving dinner with his parents."

"Then what?"

"Then we'll come back to Boston." She looked at me. "No?"

"No. Listen, I'll call my mother and tell her to have you and Sheila and Jason over on Friday night. We'll probably have turkey croquettes or something, but afterward we can go to see some movie or just sit around."

"Oh, I don't know, David. I don't think I want to be brought home to your mother so soon in our relationship." She is teasing.

"What relationship?" I raise my eyebrows. "O.K., I guess Sheila and Jason won't want to come. Anyway, it's no big deal. Please say yes?"

"Oh, O.K. I was beginning to dread being old fifth wheel. And you know New York better than I do. That's really great. Yeah!"

We go around and then head back to Radcliffe. There's an old film of Fellini's there: *The White Sheik*. I've seen it twice, but Hannah's never heard of it. She's surprised to find out it's quite funny.

98

Leaving the small auditorium, I am very conscious that I am not holding Hannah's hand and that I don't have my arm around her shoulders. Everyone else in the room seems to be touching someone else. I look over at Hannah. I don't really want to hold her hand. But at the same time, why am I thinking about it at all? We go out into the fresh air. It cuts into the lungs after all that stale smoke and subtitled Roman sun.

Hannah takes my arm. "You're a funny guy, David."

"Am I?"

"Yes," she says emphatically. "You're not very tactile."

"Oh?"

"Yes, exactly." She pauses to think. I find her hand on my arm a nice positive thing. "David. I know you're having all these problems with your roommate and his friends, and I know that you like me and you like Sheila, too, right?"

"Yes."

"But you're not using Sheila — and me — to get away from your other problems, are you?"

"It could be," I say, knowing that I was not being nice. "But I like you."

"You *like* me? Platonically?"

"Well, no. That is, I haven't had enough time to think about it." I think about it for a moment. "I like you better than spinach."

"Oh, David. Stop."

"No, really, Hannah. I care for you as a friend,

and I want to explore — to explore — to explore all the facets of our relationship . . ."

"Bullshit . . ."

". . . as they develop. But I'm not ready . . ."

"Bullshit . . ."

"I'm not ready for . . ."

"Not ready for what, David? Love? You can say the word, can't you?"

"But I'm not sure. I mean, I don't know how to recognize it. I've never been in love. I don't know what love is."

"Oh, yes you do. You must. I do. When I'm with you I know what love is."

"Oh, Hannah . . ." I protest (sounding every bit like my cousin Anne saying, "Oh mother," to my Aunt Lil). "You sound like a Doris Day movie."

I am partly angry, partly ambivalent. A small corner of my ego is pleased, but something in my superego screams caution. "Look, Hannah, I might *want* to love you. I might want to love you tomorrow or five years from now. But I don't know if I want to love you right now, right this instant. Do you understand? Please . . ."

We walk a few steps. She is looking at her feet. "Oh, David. Oh, you're right. I'm a fool and I shouldn't have said anything. I'm sorry. I'm sorry I said anything. Please erase the words. Cancel the subscription." She looks up at me, smiling bleakly.

"Hannah, let's cool it for a while, O.K.?"

We are at her residence hall. There are a few lamps glowing overhead. I can see her face. We kiss, and for the first time in my life, the kiss doesn't go away. It stays with me for hours. I can feel it on my lips as I walk back to Sheila's place.

The apartment is black and empty. Sheila's gone for the weekend again.

The smell of turpentine smacks me in the face as I open the door. I put on a record in the dark. I start to reflect. It's foolish to get so hung up on a girl. So I lecture myself on the virtues of remaining free. I tell myself that Hannah and I have some kind of relationship — maybe it's love, maybe it's a form of love. In any case, she's real and she's my — my what? My girl, my friend, my companion? Who knows? But her feelings do matter. That I know. What am I thinking, I think. I dig Hannah. I really do. If this is love, then I'm going to see it through. To the end? Must it end? Does love have to begin by being declared, like a war? Or couldn't it just creep up, like a guerrilla attack. I decide not to worry. And I try not to, believe me, with every muscle in my brain. But I stay awake until dawn not worrying.

12

THINGS ARE GETTING complicated, so I decide to go back to the dorm. Some guy tells me that his roommate has mono or some disease that made him go home for the rest of the term. So I find myself back in the bosom of college life. The past couple of weeks have given me some insight, and I find a lot of things easier going. Funny.

I still haven't written to Henry. It's been several weeks and I really should thank him for the card at least. And his birthday is right after Thanksgiving break. Must remember to buy him something — a record, probably — and give it to him when we're home. But it bothers me. Why is it that I haven't even thought about him in such a long time?

Thanksgiving break is almost here, so I give my parents a call, just to make sure I'm still welcome and that there will be the brass band waiting that I am so sure I deserve.

"Hello, Ma?"

"David! Well, my long-lost son. What's the matter, your pusher making you pay up?" My mother thinks she knows the score.

"Ha. Ha," I say flatly. "Hey listen, Ma. I'm coming home Wednesday night by shuttle flight. Is that O.K.? Can Dad pick me up at La Guardia?"

"Of course. We'll send the helicopter over. What time is convenient?"

"I don't know for sure. It's apt to be crowded."

"Let me ask your father something. He's watching the football game. Hold on a second." She leaves the phone dangling against the bright yellow walls of the kitchen. Her feet go and come on the waxed linoleum. I picture all this as I wait, surprised at how much I can't remember of a kitchen in which I've eaten hundreds of meals. She returns to the phone. "Your father suggests that you come home Tuesday if you can, and I could pick you up. Otherwise we'll get snarled up in commuting traffic and the thousands of travelers. Can you do that?"

"Sure. I have a quiz early Tuesday morning, but I can leave after that and make the eleven-ten shuttle. Are you free?"

"Yes. Free all day."

"You're really clever, Ma. Hadn't thought about cutting . . ."

"You think I didn't do anything when I was in school? Now you know. But what if that eleven-ten flight is full?"

"I'll take the next one."

"But how will I know?"

"Just before I get on the plane, I'll call you and let the phone ring three times. That'll give you just enough time to get there . . . and I can wait if you're held up."

"Gee, thanks."

"Hate to spoil your day like that."

"Spoil? What do you mean, spoil my day? I haven't seen your ugly face in two months . . ."

"Do you miss me?"

"Sure. Your insatiable appetite, your long hair, and your laundry. Oh, please bring me your laundry! I miss your little socks, your grubby underwear, your poor, your tired, your hungry masses . . ." She is laughing. "I presume that you have done your wash at least once since you've been there . . ."

"Four times."

"Four times. In two months?"

"Well, some friends of mine did it the other times."

"Such nice friends my Davey's got. What's her name?"

"Oh, Ma."

"Ah-ha! It is a girl. What's her name?"

"Ma, it isn't a girl. I mean it is a girl, but it's not what you think."

"Not what I think? She's a transvestite, maybe?"

"No, Ma, just a friend. You want to meet her? She's going to be in New York with her sister this week."

"As Aunt Sadie would say to your cousin Melvin, 'So, is she Jewish?' "

"I don't know, Ma, we don't talk about politics. Listen, she's O.K. . . ."

"Does that mean she's on the Pill?"

"Ma. Please. I wouldn't know . . . It's not that involved . . ."

"What's wrong with you? She's some kind of dog and she's got yellow teeth and bad breath? What are these kids coming to? Why, when your father and I were dating in college, I barely had time to . . ."

"Ma? Are you through? I mean, are you really through? I know all about how you and Dad are still the Romeo and Juliet of Jackson Heights, but really, this phone might be tapped and I wouldn't want this conversation to go on my confidential record. My career with the FBI and all that." I can hear my father's muted chuckling in the background. He's enjoying her half of the conversation, at least.

"O.K. So I'll see you Tuesday morning. Call me, don't forget. And tell your — ah — 'friend' that any day except Thursday is O.K. by me for dinner. Thursday there will be all those awful relatives of your father's here."

"Oh no! Not Aunt Sadie and Uncle Harold and . . ."

"Them, too. But I was thinking of the other ones: you and your brother." More chuckling from the other end.

"O.K., Ma. I've had enough . . ."

"Sure, sweetheart. You go plant your bombs, and I'll start heating the chicken soup. Bye. Take care."

"Bye. Hello to Dad."

"Yes, of course. Good-bye."

I hang up. Bombs. Even my own mother thinks about bombs. Jesus. The terrible thing is, Ted is out now with one. That I know. He and somebody else are planting one in a science lab on campus. One's timed to go off tonight. This I know from the grapevine. I've been back to the room enough to see a few things . . . torn-up notes, for one, which I put back together. One said something about a bank and I could make out "Thanksg . . ." — like maybe something was going to happen on Thanksgiving day. It's worse to know a little. I don't know enough to tip off the police, and yet I know something's going to happen. Something bad. I don't want to be labeled a traitor, either. To satisfy my conscience or whatever, I decide to try to make an anonymous phone call before I leave Boston — no questions, this way — and let the cops figure out which bank is going to be hit. Even if they don't, on Thanksgiving the banks will be closed and nobody will get hurt. Thinking about making that phone call, though, makes me feel easy.

13

Monday night I pack. I study a little, then I pack up most of my notebooks. I like my new roommate. There's nothing special about him, but he's a good influence . . . likes to study. I look forward to coming back. I decide not to fool myself about studying too much at home. Hannah will be there. And my brother. And those relatives always popping in for pastry and coffee. Reuniting. I wonder if my brother and I will ever want to do this sort of thing. Can't picture either of us with a wife and kids descending upon each other a couple of times a year. But I guess it will happen. It's inevitable.

And of course Henry will be there. What will we say to each other, I think, wondering at the same time why that ever could occur to me. Henry and I have always talked. About what? Ants, newspapers blowing in the street, baseball mitts, The Stones, jam, lampshades, typewriter erasers. What wouldn't we talk about, then? Who knows?

The bomb, a small one, went off Sunday night. It was in a laboratory, stashed under a slate counter. Evidently about all the damage done was a few broken beakers. Undergraduate stuff. The campus daily didn't make a big thing of it. It was a waste, in my opinion. Even the school administration overlooked it. Probably for insurance reasons. (They claimed that it was a chemical explosion.) Ted, of course, is angry. I run into him in the hall. He stops.

"Schoen . . ."

"Yeah?"

"Somebody's been messing with my things."

"Yeah? Too bad."

"Look, Schoen, watch out. That's a warning." And he stomps off.

The situation looks pretty bad. I've experienced all sorts of emotions, but fear is a new one with which I don't know how to cope. The weight of the phone call I had been so casually sure I would make — I'm a good guy, aren't I? Knowing the right thing makes it easy to do, no? — oppresses me through the night. In my dreams I see a baby trying to get out of one of those special jars they have in the biology lab filled with embryos. The Irish say that to dream of infants is bad luck. It means that death is coming. But death is always coming, no?

14

Tuesday morning. I go over to breakfast. Strangely, Ted is walking behind me. At first I think it's just a coincidence and he just doesn't want to get involved talking with me. So I walk slowly. He doesn't pass me. I continue. I go over to the cafeteria. I eat breakfast. Ted goes off, not too far away, with only a cup of coffee and doesn't take off his coat. He pretends to be looking out a window, but from the reflection in an unusually clean knife blade, I see him looking in my direction. I go over to my lit class and take the quiz. When I get out, one of Ted's pals is outside and he follows me back to the dorm.

I have just enough time to grab my suitcase, stashed

in a ground-floor room, and split for the car where some guys are waiting. A student is driving us over to Logan at one dollar per head. Just as we are getting into the car, Ted comes over.

"David?" He is alone.

"Yes?"

"Come here a second." He jerks his head.

"What do you want?" I ask, going over.

"Just to wish you a happy Thanksgiving."

"Same to you."

"Look, ah, I might not be here when you get back, so maybe you can have that room all to yourself."

"Why won't you be back?"

He smiles. "Well, the lawyers say that my case might be coming up and that's going to take up some time. Probably will have to talk somebody into giving me a leave of absence." He pauses. "Anyway, you can get your studying done."

At this point, his attitude abruptly changes from cordial to vindictive. "Listen, David, don't get any ideas."

"Ideas? About what?"

"Just don't," he says, looking fiercely at me.

"Look, Ted, I don't know anything. You don't have to worry about me. And you shouldn't threaten me. I'm your friend, whether you like me or not. I only hope that you don't hurt anybody." I give myself away. "Be careful."

He smiles slightly. "You know, one of the guys in the car will be watching every move you make at the airport. So don't try to call the cops. You might suddenly feel a pinprick and then it will be all over. A nice present for your parents, no? They say an overdose is a nice way to go." He gives a little shake. His hair falls to one side. His skin is pale, his blue eyes defiant.

I turn quickly and climb into the car without looking back. We leave. I look at these strange faces next to me. We don't know each other, so there's very little talk. Which one is the guy with the needle? Thinking about dying is nauseating, but a death so kind to me would shatter my parents' faith in me. Death doesn't lie, to parents. It would make failures out of them, something hideous in the eyes of the rest of the family. No bank is worth that.

I am so nervous I am shaking. Maybe Ted was bluffing. This calms me a bit. I start to rehearse what I will do when we get to the airport. An unnecessary preoccupation, but it has a soothing effect. I think about buying the ticket, getting on the line at the gate, and all that. Suddenly, I remember the phone call that I have to make to my mother. If I skip it, it might mean a lot of explaining when I see her and unnecessary inconvenience all around. I think for a couple of minutes.

In a surprised tone, I announce a bit too loudly, "Hey, I need a dime to make a call to my mother. Anybody got change of a quarter?"

Nobody answers. Finally one guy turns around and says, "I only have twenty cents. Can you use that?" I nod. "How can you possibly call your mother from Boston with a dime?"

He's the one, I figure. How else would he suspect that I didn't live in Boston? Then I remember: we're going to an airport. Obviously we are all a long way from home. I smile nervously. "I call and she lets it ring three times and then she knows I'll be on the next flight. Takes her as long to get to the airport as it does for the plane to get down from Boston."

"You live in New York, don't you?" He's looking at me in a funny way.

"Yes."

"What's the best way of avoiding the traffic if I want to get to Grand Central?"

"There are a number of things. Take the bus. It goes straight in."

"Any quicker ways?"

"That depends. If you can get over to the Flushing line, the subway can take you in. Or if you've got the money, you could take a cab."

"All the way?"

"Where are you going?"

"New Rochelle."

"That's not so far. Take a cab or one of those long airport limousines."

"That's a good idea. Thanks." He turns back to the view in monochrome zipping along past the windows.

The airport isn't too crowded, although I must say we're not the only students cutting classes in Boston. We get seats and this other guy holds my place in line. I do my phone thing and return just as the line is moving into the plane.

We land pretty much on time. There seem to be hundreds of students in the terminal. I wait until the crowds thin a little. I have no idea where to look for my mother. The information desk is crowded by students waiting for their friends. I find a phone that is working and call home. There is no answer, which is what I expect.

I wait around. The guy who was in the car with me is also making a call. I'm standing nearby and I hear him say, "See if Ruth can meet me." It was more like an order than a request. When he hangs up the phone, I join him in walking toward the doors. I'm getting warm.

"Who's Ruth?" I ask, just to say something.

"She's my mom's, um, housekeeper. Black. Funny as hell. She gets a big kick out of driving my mother's Mercedes." He smiles benevolently. "Right around the station there's this, you know, slum. And she knows a lot of people there. Gives her a big charge to drive through the old neighborhood. She's a very good driver. Never gotten a scratch on the car or any tickets. She's cool."

This sort of makes me a little ill. I am gratified to see my mother, looking small — I guess that's what being away does — and timid in the midst of all the confusion. She's about 100 feet away when she spots me. She begins to wave, and walks without looking. She is wearing an appropriately maternal plum-colored wool suit and a beige hat. I get the feeling I'm looking through the wrong end of a telescope . . . I've never realized that to someone else my mother is

113

just another person. A pretty lady, but other than that, just another person. I wonder what my father will look like to me when I see him tonight.

Dodging in and out of the crowd, we finally reach each other. The other guy must have cut out for the taxi. I give her a big kiss.

"Well, well. Kissing your mom's back in style, again, I see." She is referring to my embarrassment in September when she insisted on kissing me goodbye in front of the dorm. She pulls at my hair in the back. She's about to say something, and then she stops. "No, David, no matter how much it kills me, I am not going to say another word about your hair."

"Terrific. I may go to the barber's anyway."

"Really?" She takes my arm and we start to go out toward the parking lot.

"Yeah, Angelo still owes me some money on a bet we made on the World Series."

She hugs my arm a little tighter. "Ah, David. It's so good to have you home. Your brother is such a mensch now that he's in graduate school. He studies all the time. He's neat. He brushes his suits, polishes his shoes. He learned how to pick up his socks. He doesn't *need* me anymore!"

"How's Dad?"

"Fine. Fine."

"How's your course coming?" My mother is working determinedly toward her Master of Arts in Education.

"It's so easy. All common sense. Your father is a scream, though." We reach the car and she's unlocking the doors. "He's getting nervous about having two grad students under the same roof. Inferiority complex. His law degree may no longer be enough. He dug it out and had it framed, you know. As a joke. Sort of." We get in and fumble with the seat belts. My bags get tossed in the back. We start up. "It's a shame he's always so busy. I wish I could drag him away on vacation over the holidays."

"Where would you go?"

"Someplace exotic. The Bahamas. Ah. We won't go."

We continue along mostly in silence. When we get to the apartment, she pulls over. "O.K. Hop out here with the bags."

"It's not dangerous for you to go down into the garage alone?"

"Come on, David, I do it every day!"

"O.K., liberated lady, but it's just as easy . . ."

We drive down into the dark garage. I lug my bag to the elevator. When the door opens, out steps a thin young guy, every hair in place, his Italian shoes polished, back straight under his shiny leather coat. He says hello warmly to my mother. As the doors close and the elevator rises, I am smiling.

I smile silently for a few minutes before my mother, who is trying not to smile, says, "He's really very nice, David. He just moved in across the hall. Some kind of designer. Jewelry, I think. Sometimes he comes over for tea when he gets lonely."

"Maybe he's in love with Jim."

"Your brother is not too subtle, my dear. Don't

laugh at him; it's not funny. He's a nice person. And he's very successful in his business. But why he likes to talk to me, I'll never know."

"Maybe you remind him of his mother."

"God forbid. He told me all about his childhood. His mother sounds like an old whore. She kicked him out when he was fourteen. Lock, stock, and barrel. Luckily a friend of his took him in and sent him to art school." We get out of the elevator and walk toward the apartment. I am eager to get inside and smell the great fragrance of home. "It's odd," my mother says as she puts the key into the lock. "From his face, you would think sorrow had never touched him. It's so unlined. So serene. It hardly has any character to it, yet he certainly suffered a great deal as a child." She sighs as the door finally swings open.

Everything is more or less the same. A few more magazines. One new print on the wall. It's an etching. I decide I like it. "Oh. One thing has changed," my mother says, as though she can read minds. She puts our coats away in the hall closet. "Your brother switched your room around and he's living in the guest room. Since we don't have any guests and you're never here anyway, it's no problem with me, but I hope that you don't mind. I've been doing some sewing in your room so don't be surprised to find a few dresses hanging in there."

"Did he leave the stereo equipment there?"

"Some of it. He bought a few more parts and gismos and now the whole house is wired up. It's very exciting. Even the bathroom has a speaker. Last night your father stepped out of the shower and Jim was playing some Shinto temple music. I mean . . . you know how that sounds . . . like a glass of ice, melting? Well, Dad thought he had gotten water in his ear and for ten minutes he was bending over knocking his head trying to get rid of the ringing." She shook her head in mock dismay. "Go put your things away. I'll make lunch. Some soup and a grilled cheese. How about that?"

"Terrific. Gourmet lunch."

"All right, all right, for seventy-five cents I'll throw in some ratatouille."

15

AFTER LUNCH, I go back to my room. My room now. It's pleasant. Jim will be home in two hours, but he'll let me play what I want anyway. I never made a fuss when he came home from college. I put on some music that my mother enjoys. Schubert, Mozart, and Chopin. And I slipped in a Judy Collins album, too. I decide to review my chem notes. It is raining and the afternoon passes slowly.

A light goes on. I open my eyes. I am on my bed. I have been dreaming about Hannah and the Empire State Building and having my wisdom teeth pulled out. How Freudian can you get?

Jim is standing in the doorway. "Hey, kid. Good to see you. Sorry to wake you, but it's getting close to dinner time."

"Hey! How is everything?"

"Ah. This stuff is not so bad. No more of those disjointed undergraduate courses. Everything is interesting. Some is even exciting."

"Great." I yawn. "Hey, listen . . . I'd better take a shower. I'm still half asleep."

"Sure. Just hurry it up. Whatever it is, dinner smells good. Something tomato-y."

Jim closes the door gently. He's quiet, like he must have been when they brought me home from the hospital. A restrained discipline that a five-year-old chafes under. All that was in the click of the shutting door.

I go to take my shower. The bathroom is clean. It smells of shaving cream and ammonia. It is tiled in Jackson Heights pink, a very special color only found in the spectrum of Queens light. A muted, pale, grayish pink.

I undress, heaping clean and dirty clothes together. The water runs over me. Everything is shut out. I start to think about Hannah. About what to do tonight. Maybe nothing. Maybe just sit around until we're all sick of me, then tomorrow will be mine. New York will be mine again. The only city in the world will be mine once more. I wonder when Henry will come home. I want to go out to Staten Island with him. Taking the ferry for us was like when movie Indians become some white guy's blood brothers. It's hard to explain. There are so many things I have to talk about. I start to remember that phone call I should have made. With a sigh I get out of the shower. Through the steam and the pink tile and the doors and the wall-to-wall carpeting comes the pungency of tomato sauce.

I dry off and hurry to the close nervous scrutiny of my family.

16

It's Wednesday morning. I wake up to the strong aroma of coffee — like music. I throw on my bathrobe and shuffle out to the kitchen. It is 8:00 and my mother is fixing some scrambled eggs and leafing through recipe books at the same time. It is obvious that she has tomorrow's dinner on her mind already. My brother is there sipping coffee absent-mindedly while reading a paper he has to present at his seminar later this morning. Dad's still shaving. We can tell because the small Japanese TV set, glowing like a crystal ball on the table, is slightly distorted with little lines running horizontally through the picture. When

Dad is through, the lines stop. The "Today" Show is on. This is the news TV. (The other big one in the living room is the football-game and entertainment TV.) Anyway, the national news is being broadcast. I am looking over Jim's shoulder while I shake up the orange juice. I am barely listening.

"No!" My mother says, reaching for the volume button. "Shh . . ." she admonishes, pointing at the screen.

". . . which ripped through a First National Bank yesterday afternoon apparently has claimed the lives of four persons and injured seven. Among the dead are two bank employees, Margery Lee Bowles and James Garcia. The other persons have not yet been identified, although it is believed that two of the victims were carrying the bomb into the bank when it went off. A witness to the explosion told police that he saw two young men enter the bank as he was leaving. The pair, possibly students, were carrying a large box. 'It struck me funny,' the witness said. 'The box was from an expensive haberdashery and these young men were not at all the type to shop there.' He went on to say that they both had unusually long hair. In the witness's words, 'One was blond and his hair caught my eye. For a moment I thought he was a girl!' Boston police are searching through the rubble for clues. Names of the injured have not yet been released, pending notification . . ."

"Careful, Dave!" Jim shouts.

I almost drop the jar of orange juice. I am numb and I don't know how to react. My family is talking

122

to me, about how awful it is, and I can't respond. I sort of eat. I don't say anything. I finish breakfast and go back to my room to get dressed.

I take the subway to Grand Central. I go up to the street via the Pan Am escalator. I feel as though I have died and am ascending to paradise. Too bad Milton didn't know about this, I think, then I remember Henry and the squirrel. It is impossible to think logically. I keep trying to convince myself that Ted is dead. And in between this struggling dialogue come pictures of Henry past, present, and future, flashes of Hannah dressed in jeans and beads, then Hannah in a wool dress, her hair pulled back in a bun, pearls in her pierced ears, pearls around her neck, stockings, and expensive shoes. That's what's going to happen on Friday, I think. Hannah will be someone else when I go to meet her under the giant Kodacolor in Grand Central.

I look back down at the vomit of people flowing across the floor of the terminal. They never look up, I think to myself. I'm the only one in this whole funky city who knows that the constellations are painted on the ceiling of the terminal. Ted doesn't know. He'll never know because he's dead and he's never been to New York. Imagine being dead. Imagine being dead before you've seen New York. Impossible. I convince myself that it is so impossible to have died without seeing New York that Ted couldn't possibly be dead.

As I stumble off the escalator which is pushing me more or less along with some residual energy, I turn to look around. Same old place. Same old exciting feeling of space. Of freedom. I think about Hannah, Hannah of the slim wool dress and the tidy hair, the pearls in her pierced ears, delicately dancing from her ear lobes as she laughs, for she will surely laugh on Friday. She must. I'll make her laugh so that we can forget Ted's death. In between my fingers which are swaddled in my pockets I feel a small, folded piece of paper in one and in the other, some of those small mysterious grains of sand which creep into every pocket of every coat I have ever had, although I certainly never have worn a coat to the beach.

My eyes go inside the dark pocket and read some numbers: BU 8-1913. Hannah had written down the phone number of Jason's parents and had put it in the pocket herself, so I had forgotten about it. How beautiful a gesture. How oriental, almost. To write a number and put it in someone else's pocket so that he would feel the paper and wonder how it got there and have to think a minute to remember.

I have to talk to Hannah. I turn and go back behind the tall shafts of escalators which lead to the elevators which lead up and up into infinity. I go away from them to my right and sit in one of those molded black seats inside one of those clean glass booths. These are public phones with an upper-middle-class touch to them. And they are push-button. I punch out the number, noticing that, the half-tones of the melody it makes remind me of a fragment of something — Chopin? Mozart? *Rubber Soul?*

It rings. I will tell her about Ted. It's such a

124

stupid, stupid thing to have happened. I didn't really believe him, did I? He wasn't so convincing, was he, that I was actually afraid that I would be killed? He was kidding, wasn't he? I never fell for it. Never.

It rings again. She will know how I feel. How could he have died? No, he didn't die, I'm sure of it. It was someone else. Hannah will know. Someone she knows will have called her. Someone from the Boston underground. Hannah will know.

It rings again. She must answer. Hannah, if you love me, you must answer. Please. Hannah, I do love you, you know. I couldn't tell you then, but I do. Oh, please answer.

It rings again. On Friday I will show her all of my favorite corners of the city. All of them. The room full of Egyptian jewelry at the Metropolitan Museum. That one spot by the pond in Central Park. That place for coffee on the East Side — what is its name? Bonnier's, Tiffany's, Bloomingdale's . . . and of course Sam Goody's. Maybe we can go down to Chinatown for dinner at that little restaurant downstairs on Pell Street. And then the ferry. Oh, answer. Someone please answer!

It rings again. If only she would answer.

I will take her back from the ferry. We will go on the subway. It won't be too late, so it will be O.K. and we can go up to Jackson Heights and visit with my parents for about an hour. What about dinner? Oh, I'll just forget dinner at home. Maybe Saturday. Yes, Saturday would be better for dinner at home. Then it won't be so tense, so poised, everything just so, eaten properly and stiffly, no spilling on the damask tablecloth. Yes, Hannah must answer, otherwise everything will be too confused.

It rings again. Hannah, please. Ted may be dead, but we don't have to talk about that. Just about us. About what we're going to do this weekend. That's all. Just us. No Ted. And this weekend there are things I have to settle and I need you. I. I need you to help me. So you see you really must answer the phone. Can I tell her that I love her on the phone? No. Too corny. Can't tell her that I want to hold her, either. That would sound immature and . . .

It rings again. That makes seven times. Seven. A powerful number. If she answers on seven it's good. Seven will give me strength. I want to tell her that I don't want to go back to school. That I don't want to study psychiatry, psychology, psychoanalysis, nothing. I'm going to transfer. I'll go someplace to study film-making. California, maybe. And even if I fail everything this semester, I'll start all over, I'll pretend that I never was a freshman at M.I.T. Yes, I'll go back to zero and begin again. I made a mistake. Why didn't I know that before?

It rings again. Eight. No, don't answer on eight. On nine. Yes, one more ring. Then I'll hang up. Ten is bad. Nine is pure and forceful. ". . . This old man, he played eight, he played nick-nacks on my gate. Dah da da da dadidadi give your dog a bone, this old man came rolling home. This old man, he played nine, he played nick-nacks on my spine . . ."

126

It rings again. I hang up. My face is perspiring. My hands are shaking a bit. The door squeaks open and I get up and go out.

I find myself out on the street staring at the headlines on a newspaper. I am at a magazine stand. There is a photo of the bombed-out bank with little black arrows pointing in every direction. It makes no sense. That was a bank I'd been in several times to cash my parents' checks. Where were the aisle, the little rows of windows, the cute little brunette who used to smile at me as she snapped out my thirty dollars? ("Would you like fives or ones?") Was she Margery Lee Bowles?

It certainly isn't my fault, I reason, walking blankly through forests of people. I never knew before how easy it is to weep on the streets of Manhattan. People look away. They are used to seeing drunks and crazies teetering on the brink of lucidity. They must look away for their own sake, for their own sanity. I cover my tears with my hands, and turn my back to the city. I am facing the window of a lingerie shop. It is the bra mecca of the world. The most erotic things in the window are the gloves, standing beckoning me on amputated but graceful hands.

When my eyes focus on the surface of the glass, I notice that off to one side is a cop. He is a rectangle of navy blue, his stance that of a strong, patient man. A Chinese mandarin, perhaps. He probably thinks I'm on acid. I turn toward him and he takes a few square steps toward me. "What's the problem, kid?" the pagoda says.

"I'm O.K. It's just that my roommate was just killed."

"You at school?"

"Um."

"Accident?"

"Yeah."

"Car?"

"Umhum."

"Know how you feel. Want some coffee?"

I nod, while blowing my nose. We go into a Chock Full O'Nuts around the corner. We sit at the counter. We both order coffee and doughnuts. His coffee is black.

"It happened in Ohio on his way home." What am I saying, I think. It's one thing to lie, but to involve Henry in this . . . what if I cause him bad luck? "Happened a few days ago. I just heard about it. I just can't believe it happened."

"Yeah. It's tough, I know. A young guy getting killed." He sips his coffee slowly. "Just two weeks ago I lost a cousin. Young kid. Came back from the Nam. Not a scratch on him, you know. Joins the force. Still a rookie, see, when this happens. Gets shot one day by a sniper in Brooklyn. My aunt, she's real shook up. When you get to be my age, though, you lose a lot of friends one way or another. I got an easy beat, now. Mostly stores getting hit or parking tickets. Ah, I don't know. All these crazy radicals. Panthers, Weathermen. I got two kids." He pauses for his final sip of coffee. "I just don't know." He looks at his watch and starts to slip off the stool. "Ah, don't let it get you down, kid." He pats me on the back. "You feel better?" His shaggy eyebrows lift.

I smile. "Thanks a lot."

He smiles back. "Sure, kid." He plunks a quarter down on the counter. "So long."

"See you," I reply as he leaves. I finish my coffee slowly, leave a quarter, and start to leave. I spot a phone.

I dial Henry's number. Funny how I've never forgotten it.

"Hello?"

"Hello, Mrs. Birnbaum. This is David. How are you?"

"Oh, hi! I'm fine, David. So you're back from school. How do you like it?"

"It's great. It's really tremendous. I really like it." Why am I saying these things, I wonder. "When does Henry get home?"

"He's taking a Greyhound from Cleveland. His letter says he's supposed to get in at three-thirty. Want to meet him?"

"Sure!"

"Great. You got plenty of time. He's coming in at the West Side Terminal. He'll be surprised, won't he!" She squeals. "You come over tonight for dinner, too. I'm stuffing some cabbage."

"Thanks. I'd love to see you. But I'd better check at home first."

"Fine. Listen, David, it's nothing fancy, so if your mother wants you home, you don't have to call me back or anything. Henry will just have more to eat."

"Thanks, Mrs. B." We say good-bye and hang up. There's lots of time to kill so I walk over to the West Side. It's pretty far and I could take the subway or the crosstown bus. Ah, but Forty-second Street is so hideously beautiful. Lots of sleazy bars and movie houses and pornographic bookstores. They all have these really raunchy things in the windows. Album covers, books, devices. I think of Henry's roommate and his Bible. I have to laugh. Of all things to make me laugh today.

I walk down Seventh Avenue through the garment district. Racks of clothes are rushing past me in the streets. I stand around. The sun struggles to make a show through the cold sooty sky. Old men and middle-aged men stand in the streets looking at the sun, talking in Yiddish. I catch a few words. I feel like I am in a foreign country. A nonexistent foreign country, though. It only exists here near Broadway and Seventh. The predominant color is black: black coats, black hats, black eyes and hair. Showroom models and receptionists slink through the melodious crowd. I see a lot of people dodge into one deli. Ah-ha! Hot pastrami. I can smell it already.

17

IT'S JUST 3:35 when the bus pulls in. I am standing there waiting. Everyone comes out. Henry's not there, or at least that's what I think at first. Then I recognize him. He's got on a fitted coat, sort of long. His hair is long but combed and he's got on different glasses. His face is lean and smooth and his body no longer looks like a sack of potatoes. His appearance smacks of European elegance. Well, I think to myself, I don't believe it.

"Henry!" I call out.

He turns and grins. "David!" His arms are outstretched. I join him in a sort of stiff embrace. We dance around his suitcases shouting nonsense at each other.

"Holy Toledo!" he exclaims.

"Holy Roman Empire!" I reply.

"Holy Thursday!" he rejoins.

We gather up his gear and go up to the subway level. "So how're you doing?" Henry asks. He is grinning widely, something he rarely did before.

"Everything's fine," I say, platitudinously.

"Hey. You're great. You really are. You came to meet me! Wow. I thought I'd have to go through this culture shock all alone."

Henry is obviously wound up. "Let's go over to the Paradise Inn and talk before going home."

"O.K.," I reply. We walk along, bumping into people, dodging pillars and signs and doorways, and talk. Well, at least Henry talks.

"School is fan-tas-tic, David, it really is. The people there are incredible. I can hardly believe they're real. There's this one guy — my best friend there — he's from Germany and he's been all around the world. We're going to go to Europe together this summer. Want to come?"

"Europe? I don't have that kind of bread."

"Oh, come on, David. It doesn't cost that much to go. When you have friends there, all that really costs a lot is the transportation. It'll be terrific."

"Yeah, it sounds O.K. Just the transportation, huh?"

"Yeah. Ask your dad. He'll say yes if we go together."

132

"I suppose." Henry is so damned *positive* about it, it is hard to disagree.

Henry then continues, "And there are charter flights that the school arranges and stuff. I'm sure they have them in Boston, too. Plenty of them. We could either go together or we could meet someplace. There's this other guy who's a friend now, Martin, who's lived in Paris for a couple of years. He's got friends near the Sorbonne who have plenty of room for us to stay. He'll be there. And then there are a few other people who're going to be there studying and we can probably sleep on their floors. David, you don't know what these people are like. Man, they've all been every place. They've turned me on to so many things I never knew existed before."

We go into the restaurant and settle ourselves at a small table in the back. The restaurant has the atmosphere of any old restaurant. Kind of Greek-ethnic, kind of shabby, kind of new. We glance at the menu. We order a large feta-cheese salad, olives, bread, and a bottle of wine. Henry then resumes his schpeil about his school and the wonders thereof.

". . . And there's this other guy who — Hey, Dave, are you listening?"

"Sorry, Henry, there are lots of things on my mind."

"You know what? At school they don't call me Henry."

"What do they call you?"

"Guess."

"I don't know."

"Come on. Guess."

133

"Ha-rr-ee," I say, mocking the ubiquitous nagging wife.

"No." His pupils dilate a bit. "*Hank!*"

"You? You're not a Hank!"

"I knew you'd say that. I just knew it."

"How did you know?"

"Because I used to be a Henry. Now I'm a Hank."

"Henry, don't get me wrong, but you're still a Henry."

He looked at me blankly. "I am?"

"People don't change that much in two months."

"They don't?"

"I don't know. I never thought they did."

"You've changed."

"How the hell have I changed?"

"Well, for one thing, you're depressed as hell and you're trying to play a game with me about how you're enjoying this conversation. There's something on your mind and you want to talk about it, but you're not. You're waiting for me to stop talking. You never did that before."

"Yeah, well I'm trying to adjust to Hank. I mean, Henry's been my friend for so long, I kind of miss him."

"All right, I'll cut the bull. You tell me. What's been going on?"

The salad comes and the wine. We begin to drink. And eat. And drink. We break off in midconversation. After a few sips of wine and a dozen olives, Henry is fortified enough to continue.

"Anyway, I really like it out there and I'm glad I

134

am going there. Some kids already packed up and left. It's just not the place for everyone. You happy with M.I.T.?"

He's expecting a yes answer. I watch him carefully as I say, "No."

"No?"

"No," I repeat emphatically. "I don't know why I'm there or why I'm studying to be a psychologist. Or why I'm even in college."

"What else would you do?"

"I don't know. Get married. Run a gas station."

"Get married? To whom?"

"Nobody. It's just a hypothesis. I just don't care much what I do. I'm not certain I'm sane. How can I help anyone?"

"What do you mean? Not sane? You are utterly rational. Too much so."

"No, not anymore."

"I don't know what's been going on, but I wouldn't put down psychiatry. If you want to know about yourself you have to do it through one of two routes: the humanities or science. Even if you never put it to practical use, it's there in your head . . ."

I feel a speech coming on, so I decide to tell Henry about Ted. All the bloody details. And I tell him about Hannah. We are through our second bottle of wine and about to order another when I notice the time.

"Hey, man. It's time to go. Called your mom and she said she's making stuffed cabbage."

"Your favorite. Coming to dinner?"

"No. Your mother invited me, but I think I'll go home. Last night's grilling was enough."

"You mean parents asking questions and stuff."

"Yeah. I got it all out of my system. You haven't."

"I haven't, I guess." He smiles. "At least my *family* loves me!"

"Ah, come on, Henry. After what I've been through I couldn't take any more of that school-is-great garbage. Please forgive me."

We split the bill, leave a tip, and go back to the terminal. En route I ask, "Hey, where'd you get those nice rags?"

"Like them?" He fingers the collar on his coat. "I left my coat at home when I went to school in September, so my folks mailed it. It was stolen or got lost or something in the mail and my mother got quite a bit of money back on the insurance. It was an old coat, anyway. So she sent the bread to me and Sally and I went up to Cleveland and we bought this. It probably strikes you as being out of character, no?"

"A little bit. I wish I had one like it. It's beautiful."

"Yeah. Sally convinced me."

"How is old Sal?"

"Old Sal is terrific. Too bad she's not going to be here. Then we could have gone out together, you and Hannah and me and Sal."

"Oh, don't worry about that . . ."

"I won't. But it's a shame, anyway. Sally's the best thing that ever happened to me."

"Better than Betty?"

"Oh. I haven't told you the rest about Betty. First of all, you have to know Sally. Which you almost do. She's a very talented and unusual girl. She's holding out against my overwhelming animal magnetism, sort of a vestigial virgin of the '50s variety. Pardon the pun. Anyway, the whole thing with Betty turned out pretty ugly. A kind of charade with me as the joke. Only it wasn't very funny. There was all this talk, you know, about Betty and me. I don't know how it started, and all of a sudden I was supposed to be involved with her and some other girls — which I wasn't. Meanwhile, I was trying to live my own life and dating Sally. So all these false rumors started to filter down to her. And you know how some people are, they make everything seem so devious. I mean, Betty is a hot little piece. What am I going to do? Save myself for my wedding night? As it turns out, my extracurricular thing with Betty was also extracurricular with her. And she was talking it up in the dorms. And so all these other girls she was talking to kept confusing the situation and very conveniently let Sally know some things she really didn't want to know about me. We kept on dating, but oh man, everything I said turned against me. Finally I decided that Sally was a little high-strung and that the only way I was going to be able to put up with her nonsense was to ignore her. After a couple of weeks she asked me to go with her to the museum up in Cleveland — remember I sent you a postcard from there?"

"Yeah. The guy looked exactly like Ted."

"Yeah? I guessed. So anyway, we meet Betty up

there in the museum. She's with some funky-looking guy and she's wearing a diamond as big as a corn flake on her left hand. The guy struck me as being some kind of a jerk which is probably why . . . Anyway, Sally started to steam. I still don't understand exactly why. At the time I thought it was because she thought I was an ignoramous about art. It happens to be something about which she knows a lot and just to provoke her, I kept saying things about the paintings. Dumb things. Jokes, you know . . . treating them like cartoons with captions underneath. Jesus, she was pissed off about something. There was so much hostility after this encounter with Betty that I thought she was going to explode. Or me. Finally, after all this provocative clowning, she just started to yell at me. It was very embarrassing, actually, and the gallery was almost empty, so her voice was loud and echoing. She called me every name in the book. She wasn't actually yelling, but it sure sounded loud."

"Did she cry?" I ask, as we reach the subway platform.

"Cry? No. She just kept her teeth clenched. She was seething with jealousy. She's a very stubborn and possessive girl. She had known all along about Betty and she just couldn't take my calm introduction. She thought I was pretending that I didn't know that everyone in the school knew that I was sleeping with Betty."

"Were you?" A subway slides up and we enter.

"No. Not like it was a regular thing, anyway. It just happened a couple of times. And I never told anyone. So it had to be Betty who told someone. Anyway, Sally was jealous — though she wouldn't admit it and still won't — because she's in love with me. Still . . ."

I laughed. "You cad!" The noise of the subway is deafening as we rattle along, so we have to shout.

"Yes, but it's true. She is. And I really and truly dig her. I dig everything about her. Everything. And someday I want to — I want to have a nice constructive, enduring relationship with her." He is shouting. Suddenly the train lurches to a stop and exchanges hostages with the station platform. In a softer voice he says, "But everything works against it — these girls, her stubbornness, my stupidity. I've said the wrong thing to her so many times, David . . ." The train starts up again.

"Have you told her that you love her?" I ask, bemused.

"Are you crazy?" Henry frowns. "And ruin all the fun?"

He continues to talk but I can't hear him. My mind is wandering and so I don't even try to listen or tell him to speak up. We bump along, Henry talking and talking, me sitting there nodding. I am thinking about how I don't want to go back to school, how all of a sudden failure would be a blessing, how I want to see Hannah and get her to talk me out of whatever it is that I'm in. Scraps of Henry's chatter reach me: "Fine arts program . . . go for my doctorate in comparative literature . . . this summer . . . Sally . . . home . . . study . . . concert . . . Saturday . . . my

139

own problem . . . David . . . roommate . . . everything . . ."

Henry's stop is here. He collects his belongings and says something. Instead of nodding, I cup my hand to my ear. He's going through the door and looking at me over his shoulder. He puts a fist to his cheek. He wants me to call him, I guess. I nod and wave.

The doors close and the train pulls out slowly. I watch him as we pick up speed, envying his new confidence. Even his stride is longer, firmer, as he swings his suitcase. The train takes a curve and he's out of sight. I stand by the door. My stop is next.